THE LOVE HUNT

Andy looked at me and smiled. In that moment, the tension between us melted away.

Andy spoke first. "You're different from the other girls in school."

"You're different, too," I added hastily.

"I mean, I can't imagine talking to another girl like this," he went on. "Do you understand?"

I nodded. But Andy hadn't finished yet. "In fact, I was wondering if you'd like to get some ice cream with me tonight."

"Oh, that would be nice, Andy, but Mom wants me home tonight," I said, glancing at my watch. "In fact, I really should get going now."

He smiled shyly as he turned toward me. "Come on," he said. "I'll walk you part of the way."

Suddenly I didn't want to go home, but it was too late to change my mind.

Bantam Sweet Dreams Romances
Ask your bookseller for the books you have missed

The Love Hunt

Yvonne Greene

BANTAM BOOKS
TORONTO · NEW YORK · LONDON · SYDNEY · AUCKLAND

RL 5, IL age 11 and up

THE LOVE HUNT
A Bantam Book / August 1985

Cover photo by Pat Hill.

ISBN 0-553-25070-1

Published simultaneously in the United States and Canada

---

*Bantam Books are published by Bantam Books, Inc. Its trademark,
consisting of the words "Bantam Books" and the portrayal of
a rooster, is Registered in U.S. Patent and Trademark Office
and in other countries. Marca Registrada. Bantam Books, Inc.,
666 Fifth Avenue, New York, New York 10103.*

PRINTED IN THE UNITED STATES OF AMERICA

O   0 9 8 7 6 5 4 3 2 1

The
Love Hunt

Chapter One

Matt Duncan was the first to notice. Matt was always first at Jefferson High. He was the star outfielder on the baseball team, brash, incredibly clever, and the most gorgeous guy in the junior class, at least in my opinion.

The sun had broken through the spaces in the venetian blinds in Miss Fletcher's Biology II class, right into Matt's gleaming blue eyes, causing him to squint a little. But he didn't mind, not after a solid week of cold New Jersey rain. "All right!" he yelled, waving a fist triumphantly in the air. "Marshall High, here we come!" Matt had fidgeted all week as rain canceled a baseball game and practices day after day.

Matt's outburst paved the way for everyone else to proclaim a personal welcome to the return of sunshine. With a toss of her long, wavy blond hair, my cousin Amy turned in her seat and blew a kiss to Jason Dunbar, her latest boyfriend. I cheered along with my friends Jill Lobel and Marilyn Hall. Matt and Jason walked to the windows and began opening the blinds one after the other as everyone watched and clapped—everyone but Andy Chevalier, who sat in his front row seat, book open, waiting for class to continue.

"Class! Let's have quiet! Settle down!" Miss Fletcher shouted. Nothing short of a disaster would ever take our teacher's mind off the more important concerns of biology. She nearly went crazy whenever anything caused her to veer from her carefully planned schedule. But she was no match for the pent-up energy of thirty-five restless students.

I guess Miss Fletcher got tired of yelling. Maybe she was afraid of making herself hoarse. After a couple of minutes of our unrestrained shouting, Miss Fletcher stopped pleading, walked to Matt's desk, picked up his unopened biology textbook, and threw it back on his desk with a clap.

The noise stunned everyone. The room grew silent. Jason and Matt, who had just opened the last blinds in the rear of the room, slunk back to their seats. Matt gave me a friendly pat on the head as he passed, making my scalp tingle and raising my hopes as he had so many times before.

Miss Fletcher walked calmly back to the front of the room. "I have a special outdoor project lined up for this weekend's homework assignment," she announced. The class erupted again, this time with groans.

"Aw, Fletch," Matt complained above the general commotion. "Have a heart, will you? We're a week behind in baseball practice."

Miss Fletcher placed her hands firmly on her hips. "I fail to understand what baseball has to do with biology," she answered him. "Now if you will please quiet down."

It struck me as funny that Matt should talk about having a heart. I'd been in love with him since the New Year's Snow Ball when he'd danced with me three times and hinted at the promise of more to come. He had never delivered, and my heart nearly broke, but that didn't diminish my love for him. Neither did his endless string of girlfriends. He practically never dated a girl more than twice. But I could look at that as a good sign, as if he wanted to get everyone else out of the way first before devoting all his time to me. I was willing to wait for a boy as popular, handsome, and funny as Matt.

"Did you hear my question, Erika?" A

3

voice suddenly sounded through my daydream. I saw Miss Fletcher's beady eyes focused right on me. Jennifer Kelly and Amy turned and giggled; Jason Dunbar smirked; and Matt just looked at me curiously. I played nervously with the wispy hairs at the back of my neck.

"Would you please repeat it?" I asked. I wished I could have come up with something clever, as Matt would have done. Instead I got embarrassed. Feeling my neck go red, I turned slightly in my seat, hoping to hide the telltale sign of my discomfort from Matt.

"Since your thoughts have already drifted outdoors," Miss Fletcher admonished, "I'd like you to explain the benefits of this project to the class. Matt Duncan, in particular, seems to be under the impression that biology interferes with baseball."

The class was waiting for my answer. Out of the corner of my eye I could see Matt staring at me. I had to say something fast. "I think an outdoor project would be fun—especially now that the sun's out," I said quickly, wondering if Miss Fletcher had already announced what kind of project it'd be. Matt snorted in mock disgust and looked away. "But why not excuse anyone in sports? Jefferson High needs to win this year, and we're behind."

Miss Fletcher nodded her head. "Very diplomatic, Miss Johnson," she noted. "But unacceptable. Andy, let's hear what you have to say."

A couple of kids moaned softly. Andy Chevalier was the class brain, one of those guys who took schoolwork very seriously and always had the right answer for any question. More than once he'd pulled everybody's grade down by getting a hundred on a test graded on a curve. "Since we're studying ornithology this week," he said, "a field observation might help bring the subject to life. Birds really are fascinating creatures."

"So are bookworms," growled Matt. "But we don't study those."

"We're going to dissect worms next week," Miss Fletcher said, completely misunderstanding. The class burst out laughing, and she looked puzzled. But Andy understood, and he turned as pink as I had. The remark was unkind, but it was true. He wasn't exactly unattractive. But with his pale complexion and serious expression, Andy looked as if he spent his days cooped up in a library. He probably never spent time outdoors, playing sports as the other guys did.

Amy caught Jennifer's eye and mouthed the word "ornithology." They both giggled. I felt a little sorry for Andy, but he really had brought it on himself. Why did he insist on sounding like a dictionary?

Meanwhile, Miss Fletcher had inadvertently managed to create another commotion.

"That's enough!" she shrieked. "This is not a recess. I just wanted to see if some of you were awake." She looked at me, and I lowered my head in shame. To Matt, she said, "I think it might do you some good to see a bit of nature beyond the sports field. You might even discover that not all grass comes equipped with white stripes or baseball diamonds."

"Home run!" cheered Jason Dunbar. The class joined in again, whistling and clapping. This time even Miss Fletcher looked pleased. A smile spread across her bony face as she surveyed the class. "All right," she began, "now that we've had our fun, let's go on to the project. We've wasted enough time already." She proceeded to outline the weekend's homework assignment. "You will each be assigned one bird to observe. I want you to detail everything—what it looks like, its nest, eggs, food supply, habitat. Check out a bird book and a pair of binoculars from the biology lab if you don't own them yourself." She went over the list of common New Jersey birds.

When Miss Fletcher had finished, I couldn't help thinking to myself, *Birds! What can I possibly learn from standing around looking at birds?* Matt was right: baseball was more important. It built character and school spirit.

The baseball diamond also happened to be where most of the cute boys in school could be found. Spending my weekend in the bleachers, examining the habits of the team, would be far more enlightening than "ornithology." Unfortunately I didn't think Miss Fletcher would give me credit for studying the physical markings of an outfielder.

Sighing, I cupped my chin in my hands as she walked over to Amy's desk and handed her a white shoe box to pass around. Recently Miss Fletcher had selected my cousin as her favored assistant. With her long blond hair, round face, bright blue eyes, and turned-up nose, Amy looked like an angel who could do no wrong. But having shared a room with her for the past seven weeks while her mom was away on her honeymoon, I knew better. When she wanted to, she could be an absolute horror. I could have told Miss Fletcher a dozen stories about my cousin's treachery, including a couple about how she'd dated two boys in one night. But neither Miss Fletcher nor anyone else would bother to believe me. Miss Fletcher excused Amy from dissecting frogs because she told her the smell of formaldehyde made her sick. My mom kept telling me, "Now remember, honey, Amy's going through a rough time right now. First, the divorce. Now, her mother's remarriage. It's got to be tough on her." Everybody, it seemed, was determined to believe that Amy was a wonderful kid just going through a rough time.

But I hadn't seen her good side for a long, long time now, and I often wondered if the cousin who had been like a sister to me for so long had disappeared from my life forever.

I watched as she stopped at Andy Chevalier's desk and waited for him to choose one of the slips of paper on which Miss Fletcher had written the name of a bird. I prayed silently for a robin or a house sparrow, which were the only birds I'd ever really noticed. Andy probably knew them all. I saw him pluck a note from the box with his long, slim fingers and attempt a shy smile at Amy. Was he trying to be friendly, or did he have a secret crush on her? A lot of boys had crushes on Amy this year. But Andy's actions weren't as obvious as Matt's or those of some of the other boys. For his sake, I hoped it wasn't a crush. Amy had once told me that a boy like Andy just didn't have it—whatever "it" was.

An unpleasant thought struck me. Was I one of those girls who didn't have "it" with boys? The thought unnerved me. I looked at

Miss Fletcher with her thin, nervous lips and the unruly hair that she kept tied back in a bun to control the frizz. She probably never had whatever "it" was with men, either.

I chased the thought from my head. It didn't do me any good to think so negatively. My datelessness probably had more to do with my obsession with Matt than with any short-comings on my part. But I wasn't ready to give up. Every time I reached the brink of deciding that it was useless to hope any longer, he'd wink at me or pat my head or even just smile in my direction, and my resolve would crumble.

Andy sensed my gaze and glanced back at me with that same half smile still on his face. We both looked away quickly. I pretended to run my hand through my layered brown hair. What if Andy got the wrong idea? Once, Jennifer had hinted that he might like me. The last thing I needed was to be tagged with a boy like Andy! Then I could certainly kiss my hopes of going to the junior prom with Matt goodbye forever.

Meanwhile Matt had the class in an uproar again. Picking a note from the box that Amy held in front of him, he opened it as gingerly as if it came from a fortune cookie. "Wow, look what I got!" he exclaimed, holding the paper in front of him. Everybody turned to him expectantly. Out loud he read, "Jennifer Kelly, 682-3451." Jennifer gasped, Amy giggled, and Matt clapped a hand in front of his mouth in mock horror and rolled his eyes. "Oops! Wrong note!" he exclaimed.

Jennifer reached over and grabbed the slip from his hands. "That reads 'crow,' you nut!" she said. But she smiled broadly, flattered to have been chosen for a leading role in Matt's current act. I felt a lump slowly lodge itself in the bottom of my throat.

Jason took the opportunity to call out, "Hey, we're studying birds, not chicks!" To which Jill Lobel retorted, "Watch what you're saying, you sexist!" Again Miss Fletcher tried to restore order. Lucky for her, the bell signaling the end of the period rang.

"Please wait until everyone has received a bird!" she called out into the chaos. But it was already too late. Matt had grabbed Jennifer's hand, and I watched her dark ponytail bob out of sight as they ran out into the hall. The lump that had been forming in my throat dropped with a thud into the depths of my stomach. I couldn't believe it—was Jennifer Kelly to be Matt's latest?

I'd waited patiently through his other flings, but I never suspected my new rival would be my cousin's best friend. When would my turn finally arrive?

I stared at my desktop, wishing that what I'd just witnessed would turn out to be an illusion. If things went on like this, I'd have graduated from high school before Matt ever got around to me.

Amy had arrived at my desk with Miss Fletcher's shoe box and stood impatiently, waiting for me to grab a slip.

"Hurry up!" she urged. "I didn't finish my English homework last night, and I've got to do it during lunch."

Hardly sympathetic to her plight, I reached in among the slips, still thinking about Matt and Jennifer.

"Come on, will you!" My cousin scowled at me, shifting her weight over on one hip.

"OK, OK," I said. "But tell me about Jennifer and Matt. Since when has that been going on?"

"How am I supposed to know?" she demanded, scowling. "I don't keep tabs on them."

"Jennifer's your best friend, isn't she?" I reminded her.

"So?" Amy refused to commit herself. "You know her, too. You can ask her yourself." She picked a white slip and held it out to me. "Here—this is as good as any."

"Never mind, I got one myself." My fingers closed on a slip near the bottom of the box.

"Thanks for your info. You're a big help," I added sarcastically.

Amy sighed dramatically. Since she dated Jason, Matt's best friend, I'd once asked her to arrange a double date. But she never did, and for all I knew she hadn't even tried.

"Grow up!" she said, before tossing her hair off her shoulder and moving to the next person.

My eyes filling with tears, I got up and gathered my books together. Amy had moved on to Jill, laughing as if she suddenly had all the time in the world. I didn't understand it. When we were kids we were best friends, but ever since we'd been in high school, she'd treated me as if I were a second-class citizen. Now that she was living in my room for the semester, it was even worse.

Through the blur in my eyes, I just managed to notice that the little slip of paper with the bird's name on it had slipped from my hand and taken wing across the room. It floated neatly through the rays of sunlight on the breeze wafting in through an open window. Finally it settled on the floor across the classroom. *Oh, no,* I thought. Now I'd have to go hunting for it. I really wanted to dash to the girls' room for a tissue. Hastily I dabbed at my eyes with the back of my hand, hoping nobody would notice.

"Hey, whose bird?" a boy called out. He picked up my slip and waved it in the air. It was Andy.

"It's mine." I held my hand up, blinded by my tears. I was relieved it was him and not somebody else who found the note. Andy would never notice my red eyes. No doubt he was already in his own world, planning his bird project.

Stumbling a little as he made his way through the seats, Andy approached me with the paper. "You've picked a lucky bird," he told me, smiling sweetly as he walked right up to me. I was struck with how much better he looked close up. Of course, next to Matt, he'd wilt like day-old lettuce.

"Oh, really?" I replied automatically. I hoped Andy wasn't going to trap me into one of his educational speeches.

"Really," he echoed, holding the slip before me. "You picked a bluebird, see? Don't you know? It's the symbol for hope, love, and happiness."

"Hope, love, and happiness!" I repeated contemptuously. "Is that supposed to be a joke?"

I think it was then that Andy noticed the tears in my eyes. At least that's when he began to get flustered. He stepped back and stumbled over a desk. He looked so vulnerable just then that I couldn't help but wonder how much courage it had taken him to say those words.

Dumbfounded, we stared at each other for an awkward moment. Then we turned and ducked out of the class through two different doors.

Chapter Two

My mood had lifted a bit by the time school was over. Surely I'd made too much of that scene between Matt and Jennifer! One little flirtation with Jennifer didn't have to mean anything. Hadn't he patted my head on the way back to his desk in biology class? No doubt he'd stroll into Joe's Franks after school as free and easy as he usually was, ready to flirt with every girl in sight. If so, I wanted to be there for my share. Once, I'd treated him to my french fries, and he held my hands between his in mock gratitude. I actually didn't wash them for the rest of the day.

Joe's Franks wasn't really such a great-looking place, but the hot dogs were cheap, and since Matt hung out there after school, I did, too. A lot of juniors went to Joe's to recover from the rigors of a day at Jefferson. Joe was a nice, friendly guy—he turned the jukebox on for free and didn't care how many people shared the same meal.

Joe's was crowded when I opened the door, but I managed to grab a stool. There was an unwritten rule at Joe's that couples got booth seats, while singles sat at the long Formica counter that ran the length of the diner.

A crowd of girls huddled together at the far end of the diner. I knew what it was all about. Amy was holding one of her "therapy" sessions again. Listening intently were Jessica Cole, Jill, Debby Watson, Marilyn Hall, Kim Hofstra, and a sophomore who considered herself a junior. One of the other regulars, Jennifer Kelly, wasn't there, and her absence was not a good sign as far as I was concerned.

One of Amy's favorite pastimes was delivering lectures about human nature, as she called it. She loved talking about herself and her own family best, especially since her mother had remarried. Amy was moving from New Jersey, where she'd lived all her life, to her mother's husband's house in Santa Monica, California, as soon as school was out.

Amy tried to make it sound as if her

16

mother had gotten married just to make her miserable. But Aunt Carol had been unhappy ever since her divorce from Uncle Bob some years before. When she had announced the marriage, she had looked happier than I could remember seeing her. Amy had seemed thrilled, too. But when Aunt Carol took off on a three-month, cross-country honeymoon and left Amy in my mother's care, my cousin felt abandoned and let everyone know it.

Since she was living with us now, I often wondered how much info about Mom and Dad and me contributed to her gab sessions. Mom had tried to make Amy feel loved and welcomed in our home, but Amy never demonstrated any appreciation as far as I could see. She never thanked Mom for doing her laundry and always had some excuse why she couldn't set the dinner table. She didn't seem to care that I'd given up half my room for her, either; she took it over as if she'd lived there forever.

"Nobody has any idea where Mom is," I heard Amy tell the eager group as I ambled over to listen. I stopped just far enough away that she didn't notice me. "That postcard from Yellowstone National Park was the last I've heard from her."

"You poor thing," Jessica said, leaning over to pat Amy reassuringly on the arm. "How could your mother leave you alone like that?"

"It's just awful," Amy confirmed, her voice heavy with sadness. "It's like a prison in the Johnsons' house. There are rules for everything and chores every time I turn around. And having to share a room with Erika's no picnic, either." She let out a deep sigh, as if only her generous nature enabled her to endure my presence.

I could cheerfully have killed her on the spot. How dare she lie about us? Mom and Dad allowed her to do practically anything she wanted, with no responsibility and a generous curfew. She didn't even have to clean up her side of the room! I listened to see how outrageous her stories would get.

"Erika's always asking me to do things for her," she continued her complaint.

I couldn't take it anymore. "Like what?" I challenged.

Amy didn't seem embarrassed by my catching her talking about me. She shot back, "Like demanding I fix you up with Matt Duncan."

I couldn't believe I'd heard her correctly. How could she say that in front of the girls! I'd asked her about Matt in confidence, and she had sworn she'd never say a word about our conversation to anyone. Humiliated, I could feel the red rushing up my exposed neck. "I—I never demanded anything," I managed to say,

18

gaining courage with each word. "You're exaggerating, Amy, just like you exaggerated about your mother. You know she and your stepfather went on a back-country camping trip and would be out of touch. She said she'd write again as soon as she reached civilization." The other girls stared at me as Amy shot me a dirty look.

"Who asked you?" she demanded, fire spewing from her blue eyes. "Are you always in the habit of going through other people's mail?" Her pretty mouth was now an ugly scowl.

"You showed me that postcard!" I cried. "Why are you twisting the truth?"

"Is she?" Jill spoke up then. "Everyone knows what a crush you've had on Matt."

"Not that it's gotten you anywhere," Debby added snidely.

Before I could speak, Marilyn Hall stepped in. "Come on, girls, lay off!" she warned. Marilyn was always the regulating force.

Everybody looked as sheepish as I felt. When would I learn to stay out of Amy's gossip sessions?

"How about it, cousins?" Marilyn coaxed. "What do you say you kiss and make up?"

Amy smiled thinly. I could tell from the color in her cheeks that she was embarrassed by the whole scene. But I was still humiliated—all these girls knew how I felt about Matt; nothing could erase that fact. As much as I wanted in that moment to throw my arms around Amy and wipe out all the trouble between us, my pride would not let me.

"Well, I've got to go," I mumbled, hardly looking at anyone. "I'll see you guys around."

"Sure," a couple muttered in return. I knew they were relieved to see me go. The tension in that corner of the room was thick.

My face still burning, I walked back toward the other end of the diner, creeping past the bodies around me.

Joe's was still crowded. Someone turned on the jukebox full blast, drowning out most meaningful conversation. I noticed a lone boy in a booth, peering intently into a book. I wished I could trade places with him rather than return to my exposed stool. Instinctively, he looked up as I passed.

"Hi," I said automatically. It was Andy. He looked uncomfortable and out of place. Of course he wouldn't know about the booth rules.

"Want to sit down?" he asked, looking shyly over the top of a textbook, *Principles of Trigonometry*. He spoke so softly I barely heard him over the music.

"OK," I agreed reluctantly. I didn't especially want to be seen with him, but the booth was a convenient spot to wait for Matt. With the stool gone, I couldn't stand by myself.

"Would you like something to drink?" Andy asked as the waitress came closer, raising his voice to be heard over the music.

"A root beer, please," I shouted to the waitress. Andy didn't say anything else, and I began to wonder why he'd come to Joe's and why he'd asked me to sit with him. Except for our awkward meeting in class, we'd never spoken. Had he felt conspicuous sitting at the booth alone? I felt strange, too, being there with him. Andy wasn't exactly my choice of a boyfriend. I sighed dispiritedly. I was in a booth at last, and I was as lonely as I had ever been in my life. If I hadn't ordered a root beer, I would have escaped to my room at home. After a few more painfully silent moments, the drinks were served.

"What do you think of the biology project?" Andy asked as he peeled the wrapper from his straw. He tried to look into my eyes as he said it, as if he'd read a book called *How to Talk to Girls*. It was sort of touching—as though Andy lived his whole life through books and didn't really know how to act on his own.

"It's OK," I said. "I've just never learned to use a pair of binoculars before."

Andy pounced on my words. "There's

really nothing to it. If you like, I could show you how."

"Oh, no. I'm sure I can manage," I said quickly.

Andy looked disappointed. For one whole awkward moment we said nothing while we stared at the ice in our drinks. No doubt the girls in the back had seen us by now and were laughing.

"I know the class thinks birds are a waste of time, but birding is really a hobby of mine," Andy went on. "My dad's an amateur ornithologist and he's been studying birds for years. He knows as much about them as anyone."

"Really?" I asked, uninterested. My mind was on every boy that entered the diner. Sooner or later one of them would be Matt.

"Oh, yes. Birds are really neat. Have you ever heard of a puffin?"

"No." I glanced at my watch: 3:42. Matt should have been there already. What was holding him up?

"They're funny birds." Andy laughed nervously. I realized then I'd hardly ever seen him smile before. He had two deep dimples that gave him a sort of impish quality.

Quickly I turned my head toward the window. Still no sign of Matt's red pickup truck in the parking lot.

Andy chattered confidently on, oblivious

22

to my inattention. "They live on the northern Atlantic Ocean," he continued. "But, you want to hear something really neat?"

"What?"

"No one knows exactly where they go in winter. But every spring they return to lay one single egg in the area where they were born!"

"Too bad Amy's mother isn't a puffin," I commented.

Andy was puzzled. "Huh?" he questioned, squinting nervously through his glasses.

"Oh, nothing," I said. Why get him drawn into this? Then I forgot Andy altogether. Out of the corner of my eye I saw a flash of red. Matt's pickup truck had pulled up in Joe's parking lot!

"Is that what was bothering you in biology today?" Andy asked. But his voice sounded a million miles away.

I noticed that Matt had emerged from the car with Jason and a girl. I couldn't yet see who she was, but I had an idea.

"In biology?" I repeated dumbly. The girl with Matt had dark brown hair, and she grabbed his arm as they headed toward the door. My eyes burned again. I had to make something up quickly.

"Oh." I looked back at Andy. "It was hay fever, if that's what you mean. I got an attack

23

at the end of class. It's been bothering me all day."

"Oh." Andy sounded unconvinced. "Look, I know it's none of my business, but . . ."

Andy's words drifted away into the background noise as Matt pushed the door open to Joe's. He breezed in, looking confident and sure of himself. *Why wouldn't he be?* I thought bitterly. Jennifer Kelly was right behind him, and on her face was a big smile that told everyone in sight, "He's mine!" My hopes were dashed again. The latest round of competition was over, and the long winter's sadness rushed over me. I had been passed by once more.

As the familiar tears welled up in my eyes, I fought to hide my face from Andy. I was trapped in the booth. I'd have to pass Matt to leave the diner or pass Amy to get to the bathroom. I wasn't about to be caught crying again. Was this what life was going to be all about for me—the constant waiting and watching while some other girl got the boy I wanted?

Andy looked straight at me. "Erika?" he asked softly, reaching for my arm.

I got up from the booth and grabbed my books. "I've got to go," I muttered. "Dentist appointment—forgot all about it."

Matt stopped me at the door before I could

rush out. "Hi, Erika, old pal," he said, grinning broadly. "Think your friend the bookworm over there would give Jennifer and me his booth? Joe's rules, you know." *You might have shared a booth with me,* I thought.

"Ask him," I managed to rasp. I didn't want him to see my face. Or Jennifer, either. I squeezed past them and out the door.

It was only after I'd gotten within a block of my street that I realized I'd stuck Andy with the tab for my root beer.

Chapter Three

As soon as I got home, I ran upstairs to my room and flung myself on the bed, ready to indulge in a good, private cry. But a sudden sharp pain in my ribs left me sitting up in surprise. Amy's travel hair dryer had been left on my handmade quilt. As usual, she hadn't bothered to put it away after she'd used it. Disgusted, I flung the dryer across the room onto her unmade bed, which wasn't even supposed to be a bed at this time of day. It was my convertible love seat, and during the day it was meant to stand closed up into a couch with a little pillow at each end.

Until Amy's arrival, the love seat had stood by the window and had been my favorite place to sit and read. Now I was lucky if it was ever a love seat at all. The freshly washed sheets that Mom had put on just the day before were crumpled and had been soiled when Amy had spilled some powder blusher on them.

A jumbo towel, still damp from her morning shower, lay in a heap on top. The least Aunt Carol could have done for her daughter before she left was to teach her how to clean up after herself, I thought grimly.

Immediately I felt guilty. Mom had reminded me daily for seven weeks that I was the lucky one and that I had to be patient with Amy. She'd practically drilled the words into me: "Remember, honey. It's hard enough when a parent remarries and you barely know your new stepparent, but then to have to move away from the town you've lived in all your life—where all your friends are—now, that's rough! Amy needs all the understanding we can give her."

Of course, I knew that was true. But it seemed just as true that Amy wasn't having a bad time at all, while I was miserable. My cousin was beautiful and popular; I was dateless and lonely. Amy had Jason, and I wanted a boyfriend, too—one who needed me as much as I needed him. A boy whom I could tell all my secrets to, who would understand me and love me in a way nobody else had before. It could be

Matt, if only he would wake up and see that I was the right girl for him. Jennifer was destined to be just the latest on his merry-go-round of girls. I could care for him deeply and genuinely. I would be the one who would last. But would Matt ever realize that? I would never know until I had been alone with him. But would that day ever come?

I sat up, cupped my face in my hands, and sighed a long sigh, full of self-pity. Usually when I daydreamed about Matt, I'd stare into my dresser mirror. This time, though, no image gazed sympathetically back at me because Amy had chosen the corner of my mirror as the resting place for her bathrobe, and the flannel material obscured most of the glass. I wondered why she'd bothered to hang it anywhere; most of her other things were strewn all over the floor. I fit my face neatly into the little patch of mirror still exposed. Except for a few wispy ends, my hair didn't show. It was growing out from a layered cut and was a disaster in contrast to Amy's flowing locks. At least my face was pleasantly heart-shaped—inherited from Mom—and my skin was smooth and clear.

But then there was my nose. I bent it back and forth with my finger. Why couldn't I have a little turned-up nose like Amy's? I laughed when I remembered complaining about it to

Dad, who said, "I think your nose is just fine." It was then that I noticed it was exactly like his. Only it looked an awful lot better on a forty-five-year-old man than on a sixteen-year-old girl.

My eyes were my best feature. Mom always called them "chameleon eyes." When I was little, I used to ask her, "What color are my eyes today, Mom?" Then she would answer "blue" or "green" or "gray" or "turquoise." Lately, though, we hadn't played that game. Since Amy moved in, they had remained permanently green with envy.

As if on cue, there was a knock on the door. It opened a wee crack to reveal Mom's smiling face. "Hi, honey!" she said, greeting me. As the crack widened, though, her smile disappeared.

"Oh!" she gasped when she saw the chaotic state of the room. In addition to the unmade bed and the piles of clothes strewn all over the floor, my desk and dresser were covered with books, magazines, and opened bottles of body lotion and nail polish. It couldn't have been a pleasant sight for a mother who worked all day and counted on her family for help at home.

"Good heavens!" my mother said, looking around her. "It isn't like you to be so sloppy, Erika."

"Welcome to Amy Brooks's disaster area," I remarked sarcastically. "Did you really think I made this mess, Mom?"

"Oh, Erika." She sighed and plunked down dispiritedly on the bed next to me. I knew her job at the nearby shopping mall wore her out.

"What should we do?" I asked. I meant about Amy, but she didn't understand it that way.

"What?" she answered. "Why, what do you think we're going to do? Clean this mess up now, immediately!" She jumped up and pulled off her blazer.

"Mom!" I protested. "Amy made this mess, and she ought to clean it up instead of gabbing with the girls at Joe's all afternoon."

"Erika!" She threw me a stern look. "It certainly would be nice if Amy were neater, but isn't that just a small thing compared to what she's going through?"

I made a face, but I knew better than to say anything.

"It's only been a couple of months since Aunt Carol remarried," Mom went on. "So Amy's hardly had a chance to get adjusted. And I'm sure she still has mixed feelings about Uncle Bob."

Outside of her therapy sessions, I figured Amy spent a lot more time thinking about school and boys—especially Jason—than about her father, my uncle Bob, or even her new stepfather. But I kept that to myself. Mom didn't look as though she were in a mood to be challenged. With the determination of a woman on a worthy mission, she went through the room, picking up clothes, shaking them out, and sorting them to be hung back up or go into the laundry.

"That poor child must be terrified at spending her senior year in a new school three thousand miles away. Really, Erika, imagine what must be going on in Amy's head."

But what about what's going on in mine? I wanted to shout. Mom had been so attentive to Amy's needs that she hardly ever had time to listen to my troubles anymore. We cleaned in silence for a while. As I hung up one of Amy's not too wrinkled shirts in my closet, I realized it had been a long time since I had confided in my mother. "Uh, Mom—" I began.

Mom looked up at me, and as she did she turned her head to scour the room. "Well, we've done it," she announced. To my surprise the room looked almost normal again. I wondered if Amy would notice. "I'm going to go down and start the meat loaf," she said. "Would you please finish up here with a good vacuuming?"

"Sure, Mom," I answered.

On her way to the door, she stopped and

turned around. "Oh, Erika, what did you start to tell me?"

I had lost my nerve. "Oh, nothing," I said. Mom probably wouldn't consider boy trouble a high priority item on the problem scale when placed beside Amy's adjustment to her mother's marriage.

"Remember," Mom said, winking at me before she left the room, "Amy needs special love and attention right now. It's a very trying time for her. You understand, don't you, sweetheart?"

"Yeah." I nodded. "Sure, Mom."

"That's my girl." Mom smiled approvingly, then she was gone.

After smoothing the wrinkles on my bed-spread, I started for the vacuum. As I bent down to turn it on, I noticed a slip of paper on the floor. My biology bird assignment. It seemed determined to fly away from me. "Bluebird" was written in Miss Fletcher's neat handwriting. What was it that Andy had said about the bluebird? It was the symbol of hope, peace, and happiness. The thought made me laugh out loud.

Poor Andy. He had meant well, but obviously this was one bird that had been assigned to the wrong person!

Quickly I vacuumed the room, and when I finished, I was glad Mom had made me do it. It felt good to have my clean room back, even if I hadn't been responsible for the mess in the first place. I liked neatness and order. It was hard for me to think clearly when everything surrounding me was in chaos. Now that I could see the top of my desk, I pulled my history book out of my knapsack and started to read. Thinking about the Monroe Doctrine had to be more rewarding than thinking about Matt at this point.

A loud, sudden knock at the window startled me. I looked up to see a bird lying in a daze on the sill. It must have flown into the window, I thought. Hoping it wasn't hurt, I opened the window and gently took the bird in my hand. It felt warm, and its heart was still beating, though its eyes were closed. Some chirping nearby caused me to look out. On a branch of our old oak tree stood another bird beside a nest. I knew these birds were robins. Maybe they had been looking for nesting material.

I held the limp body in my hand and stroked the red breast while its mate called anxiously from nearby. "Please don't die!" I whispered softly. The bird was a pitiful sight lying there. Yet at the same time, I was struck by the incredible beauty of its glistening dark gray head and wings. Its breast was as orange as a freshly picked fall pumpkin, and its perfectly formed feet had five tiny claws made just for scraping for worms. I hoped the bird would live. If it had babies, I'd be able to watch them through the bedroom window!

As I was about to bring the bird back in through the window, it opened its eyes and looked right at me. Its feet started to twitch. I placed it back on the sill, hoping it wasn't too hurt to return to the nest.

After looking around for a moment, the bird revived completely and fluttered over to a nearby tree branch. Its mate hopped over as if to stand guard. It would be OK.

The first smile of the day spread across my face. As if on cue, Amy walked in, slamming the door loudly behind her. She pouted when she saw me, probably remembering the incident at Joe's. If she noticed the job Mom and I had done on the room, she didn't comment on it.

"Daydreaming again?" she asked, dropping her books on the love seat.

"Huh-uh. I'm watching something."

"What's so interesting out there?"

"Oh, a bird flew against the pane just now," I answered as matter-of-factly as possible. "I brought it back to life and let it go."

"Ooh, let me see," Amy said, squeezing next to me for a look. Her curiosity surprised me.

"It's one of those birds right there." I pointed to the nest. "They'll probably have a bunch of babies soon."

"Really?" Amy leaned out and brushed her hair right into my nose, making me want to sneeze. "What kind of birds are they?"

"Robins," I said.

"Robins!" Amy turned and began throwing her books in all directions. At the bottom of the pile was her biology notebook, and she began to flip through its pages.

"All right!" she shouted, waving a small white slip in the air. "That's my bird!"

"What?" I said.

"I got 'robin'! I got robin for my bird assignment!" Curling up on the newly made love seat, she closed her eyes, pretending sleep and murmuring dreamily. "I can do my report from the comfort of my own bed!"

With another leap she was back at my side. "Gee, thanks, Erika, you're a doll," she said in mock gratitude. "Now I can go to watch Jason play this weekend. No chasing around town after those silly birds for me!" She planted a big fat kiss on my cheek.

I just stood there lamely while she bounded out the door. A second later she bounced back in again.

"Can I borrow your red sweater, Erika,

please? I've got to run over to Jason's for a sec, and I don't want to dig for mine."

"Go ahead." What could I say? It was only a sweater—and Mom's words about being understanding still echoed in my ears.

As my cousin bounded down the stairs, I heard Mom call out, "Be home in an hour, honey. Dinner will be ready then."

Once again, Amy wouldn't be helping out.

Chapter Four

Though it was only seven o'clock, the sun was shining brightly through the window when I woke up the next morning. Miss Fletcher had suggested getting an early start on the project, reminding us with a thin-lipped smile that "the early bird gets the worm." I yawned and stretched my arms up, way over my pillow. Saturdays were my days for dozing late, and I hated getting up. But Mom had promised to take Amy and me shopping at noon, and I wanted to get the project out of the way.

At least Mother Nature was making it as painless as possible for me. A wonderful scent of fresh morning air and spring blossoms filled my nostrils as I opened my window. I inhaled deeply. An incredible chorus of singing birds acknowledged the first sunny weekend of the month. The morning seemed full of hidden promises. The world was undergoing its yearly rebirth, and I wanted to be a part of it.

Jumping out of bed, I pulled on a pair of jeans and reached in the closet for a plaid flannel shirt. Over this, I put a baggy red sleeveless sweat shirt. The red brightened up my brown hair and pale complexion.

Grabbing my binoculars and bird notebook, I tiptoed quietly toward the door, taking one last glance at my sleeping cousin. She lay exactly where she'd fallen into bed the night before. While I preferred being tucked as neatly into bed as if I were inside a cocoon, Amy lay with her blanket and sheets on top of her in a heap, her arms and legs stuck out on all sides. Her mascara from the night before had smudged under both eyes so that she looked like a football player. In school Amy dressed neatly and fashionably, and her makeup always looked fresh. Her nails were perfectly filed and polished, and her hair was always trimmed and set. No one would have believed she could be such a slob at home.

I had a fleeting desire to take a snapshot of her, so I could show it around school when she got into one of her superior moods. But then I thought better of it. Mom would be furious; besides, with my luck it would probably backfire and enhance Amy's image as Jefferson High's beautiful Orphan Annie.

Miss Fletcher had told us that the birds she assigned were common, so the first place I thought I'd look was in my backyard. I sat in the still morning, focusing my binoculars on everything that flew by. At the end of forty-five minutes, I must have seen five starlings, twenty house sparrows, three house finches, and two monarch butterflies. But, oddly enough, not a single bluebird.

The robins stared at me as if they believed I was after their worms. After my rescue mission, I felt a little hurt. "You should love me, you know," I told them reproachfully. Embarrassed at my silliness, I was relieved when the birds flew away, leaving me and my homework assignment behind.

One thing about being assigned a bluebird, I realized, was that I only needed to bother with the binoculars if the bird looked blue. With that thought in mind, I decided to try the rest of the block. Perhaps bluebirds weren't wild about the Johnson backyard.

Quincy Street didn't yield any bluebirds, either, though I saw several blue jays. Actually, I think it was the same one every time. My sweat shirt probably made me look like a big, fat reddish cat, and the blue jay may have been spying on me for the neighborhood birds. His shrill scolding probably woke up every last late sleeper on the block. But it sure didn't attract any bluebirds.

I finally decided to return home, get some breakfast, and ride my bike over to Otter Pond Park at the far end of town. Clearly bluebirds didn't favor my side of the tracks.

It was nearly ten o'clock when I got to the Otter Pond Forest Reserve. Though it was called a "reserve," Otter Pond was really more like a town park. When the weather was nice, Otter Pond was a great place to pass time. Kids hiked there, families picnicked there, and developers watched it with a patient eye. One of these days, they said, Otter Pond was going to be turned into a shopping mall. I hoped not. With its thick pine woods and secluded hiking trails, Otter Pond Park was one of the few places left in town where you could go for peace and quiet. There were plenty of malls around already; lately they seemed to open one every year.

A flash of blue went by, and I made a fast grab for my binoculars. Rats—another blue jay! The little crested devil was putting the whole woods on alert. Looking around me, I wondered if any of my bluebirds were hiding out in the undergrowth somewhere. I hoped they'd tire of playing hide-and-seek soon—I wanted to get this project done with and get on with the rest of my day.

As I waited, my thoughts naturally wandered to Matt. I half hoped he'd appear from behind a tree and take me into his arms, telling me it was all over between him and Jennifer. But even as I thought it, I knew there was practically no chance of it. Amy and Jason had doubled with Matt and Jennifer the night before. My cousin had delighted in waking me to tell every last detail of the evening, including all the times that Matt kissed Jennifer. I didn't know which hurt me more—Matt's actions or Amy's deliberate cruelty. I couldn't believe this was the same girl I'd shared my secrets with when we were little. For all I knew, she'd already blabbed about them, too, in one of her sessions at Joe's.

The sound of a footstep on a brittle twig made me whirl around. *Matt!* I thought. But it was Andy Chevalier. He stood on the walk behind me, grinning with surprise. Naturally. Who else but Andy would take this project seriously?

"Hi," he said shyly. I noticed he was wearing a pair of jeans and a flannel shirt similar to mine. Over his shirt he wore one of those fishermen's vests, the kind with all those neat pockets. He was carrying an impressive-looking pair of high-powered binoculars mounted on a tripod, which he supported in his other hand.

"Hi," I answered, still glued to the spot. The passing hope that I would run into Matt had died fast. He was probably at baseball practice now. I should have figured that out earlier. Jason and Amy would be there, too. Andy was probably the only boy in school who wouldn't be tossing around a ball on a warm spring weekend. Still, he looked more rugged than he'd ever looked in class. Maybe the outdoor air did him good.

"How's it going?" Andy grinned and walked toward me. He seemed more confident than he did in school.

"Fine," I said. "There are certainly a lot of birds around."

"Yeah," Andy began. "I'm doing a house sparrow. Actually, I've already seen millions. They're so common. Do you want me to help you find your bird?"

"Nope," I answered a bit abruptly.

Andy seemed surprised. "Why not? Don't you need some help?"

"Of course not!" I insisted. Did he think I was a dummy? "I already saw one," I lied.

"You did? Where?" Andy's eyes narrowed a bit. His pupils looked darker, almost piercing under his glasses. I stepped back a bit.

"If you don't mind," I said, "I'd rather save the information for my class report."

"OK," Andy agreed, though he sounded a little hurt. "I just wasn't sure if you'd have any trouble, that's all. Bluebirds are—"

"No trouble," I interrupted. *I'd find it myself if it took me all day*, I vowed to myself. "Well, I guess I'd better get going," I said.

Standing on a forest path with Andy was a bit awkward. How different the morning might have been if I had met Matt like this. But he was at baseball practice, and I kept running in to the most unromantic boy at Jefferson High. Meanwhile, I still had my bird to find. I started to walk back to where my bike stood waiting.

"Wait!" Andy exclaimed. "I have a little secret here. Would you like to see it?"

"Well," I answered a bit doubtfully, "OK. But I promised my mom I'd be back soon." In spite of myself. I was curious to know what kind of secret Andy could have.

"Follow me," he called. "Just wait until you see this!" He turned and practically ran up a path marked Trail C. That trail was the hardest hiking path in the Otter Pond Reserve, but Andy navigated the inclines and rough spots with a sure foot. I followed, grasping at trees and gasping for breath, amazed at his energy. It was obvious he didn't learn to hike like that in a library.

"You all right?" He stopped at the top of the second hill, waiting for me to catch up.

"Sure," I said, trying to hide my panting.

"Come on!" Andy couldn't control his enthusiasm, and he grabbed my hand. I was amazed at the strength of his grip as he practically pulled me up the next hill. Why had I ever thought he was some kind of weakling? As we climbed upward into a pine forest, the trees grew dark and tall.

Just when I was beginning to doubt that Andy's "secret" actually existed, we arrived at a clearing in the woods. I sat silently on a smooth rock while Andy set up his equipment and focused on a group of trees about a hundred yards away. The air was heavy with the scent of pine, and Andy's spot was unmarked by footsteps or any other signs of human presence.

"Take a look," Andy commanded. His brown eyes were bright with anticipation as he pointed to the binoculars. The Andy I was with was completely unlike the boy who sat silently in my biology class. I flushed self-consciously under his intense gaze before squinting through the binoculars.

The vision was one I'd seen many times in movies and in magazines. But seeing it in real life was awe-inspiring. A large eagle sat, staring out from the top of a tall, dead tree. The nest he occupied could have been a tree house. I gasped in wonder.

"I don't believe it. It's a—"

"Yep!" Andy finished for me. "You're looking straight at a bald eagle."

I objected. "I thought they were extinct!"

Andy shook his head with excitement. "Not quite. DDT killed most of them, and development took care of almost all the rest, but there are a few left." He turned to me, his face one huge smile. "Isn't this the most incredible sight? Imagine having a bald eagle right here in Jefferson Township!"

"It's terrific!" I had to agree. Andy surprised me. There was an enthusiasm and a decency about him that I had never noticed before.

The huge bird had seen us and started to demonstrate its objection to our intrusion by standing upright in its nest and flapping its monstrous wings up and down. For a minute I believed it might be preparing to swoop down on us, and I cowered in panic as it flew directly overhead, warning us with shrill, hoarse cries not to come any closer to its nest. Its huge wingspread, hooked beak, and piercing eyes gave it a menacing look that made it hard for me to believe the bald eagle could be related to the small, warm robin I had held in the palm of my hand only the afternoon before. A cry of fear escaped from my throat.

I half expected Andy to stand there and laugh at my terror. Hadn't I giggled with the rest of the class whenever Matt or somebody else had made a joke at his expense? Here was the perfect chance to get back at me. We were alone in the woods, and I was at his mercy. He was clearly in control.

But Andy didn't laugh. With his eyes reflecting real concern, he did the last thing in the world I would have expected. He put his arm around my shoulder and, holding me gently, said, "Don't worry. That eagle may be big, but she's really not so different from your bluebird. She just wants to make sure we don't hurt her babies, that's all." Then, when he realized his arm was around me, he released his grip. "I'm s-sorry, Erika," he said, stammering slightly.

How often had I dreamed of a boy putting his arm around me the way Andy had done! Only the boy I had imagined it to be was Matt. Andy's embarrassment made me self-conscious as well. Parts of me went hot and others went cold, while my face flushed and then paled.

Confused and not knowing what to do, I quickly moved away from him, "Um, I, um—" I started, wanting to leave the painful scene. When I turned around, however, I discovered that the trail divided into two, and I had no idea which one we had come from. I knew I'd be lost if I set out alone. I waited uncomfortably for Andy to pack up his equipment and walk back with me.

When he had folded the tripod and joined me. I could tell by one look at his face that he was as confused as I. We walked back in silence, and though our hands touched a couple of times when he helped me over some rough spots, neither of us spoke for the fifteen minutes it took us to return to the main park grounds. I had no idea *what* to say to him. How could I possibly explain my clumsiness, my insecurity, my inexplicable confusion to Andy Chevalier?

Down at the parking area, we had nothing to say, so I mumbled, "Let me pay you for that root beer I stuck you with yesterday." I could hardly look at him as I said it.

"Forget it," he said. "What about you get me one next time?"

"Oh—sure." I agreed. *What did Andy mean by next time?*

It was then that I looked at my watch. I was late for my shopping trip with Mom and Amy. Muttering a feeble goodbye, I jumped on my bike and took off for home as fast as I could, without so much as a glance back at Andy.

Chapter Five

I pedaled home so furiously that I was completely out of breath by the time I turned into the driveway, where I nearly crashed into Dad's car. A few puddles lingered on the black asphalt from the bath the car had received earlier.

"Aunt Mary! Erika's back—*finally*," I heard Amy call. She was sitting on the front steps wearing a khaki jump suit she'd sewn in home ec—and a frown of impatience.

"What took you so long?" she asked, scowling. When she was angry, she didn't look half so pretty as everybody said she was.

"I was doing my bird-watching," I said.

"Well, some people do their homework

and also are ready when they say they're going to be," she admonished.

I felt my blood rising again, but in a much different way from how it had with Andy. Then, I'd felt peculiarly energized. My skin tingled with the memory of his touch. Now I just felt angry, and, worse, frustrated. With Mom within earshot I couldn't talk back to Amy the way she had talked to me. I had to swallow my answers.

Mom appeared at the door just then, jangling the car keys. "OK, girls!" she called to us, running ahead to warm up the car.

I wanted to go in and comb my hair and put on some makeup, but they both seemed to be in such a hurry that I didn't have the courage to ask. After all, I *was* late.

It didn't help my spirits to observe Amy. She looked terrific in her jump suit with her matching flat-heeled boots. She'd put on eyeliner and pink lipstick, too. I was barefaced, and my hair hung messy and stringy. I was still wearing my hiking boots, and a dirt smudge on my jeans told the story of my adventure at Otter Pond Reserve.

I wondered at my mother's insensitivity as she hurried me into the car. Didn't she know I'd want to change my clothes? Amy must have been pestering her all morning. If anybody I knew showed up at the mall and saw me like this . . . I sank into the backseat of the car and let myself give in to depression.

Mom must have noticed my silence as she made a right turn onto Main Street. "How'd it go, honey?" she finally asked me.

"OK," I answered. I was in no mood to admit my morning adventure had been a bust. I wondered if Amy really had done her biology homework as she'd said.

"Good," Mom answered, satisfied with my response. Obviously her mind was already on other things. She didn't pursue my uninformative answer as she usually would have.

"Aunt Mary, weren't those robins cute?" Amy interjected. Her comment seemed to grab Mom's attention.

"Oh, Erika!" she said enthusiastically. "You should have seen it. Amy discovered a nest of robins in that tree just outside your bedroom window. Can you imagine!"

"No kidding!" I said sarcastically. Mom was just being agreeable—I couldn't blame her for her pleasure. I had reacted the same way when I spotted the birds. But her total admiration of everything Amy did made me furious.

"Honestly, Erika!" Mom admonished. "The way you act, you'd think I just told you the cat ran away. What's wrong with you today?"

Amy turned and made a face. Though she didn't say a word, I could tell she wanted to know the same thing. I didn't dare say, "I'm mad because Amy looks great and I look like a slob, and I'm the one who spotted the robins, not Amy, and if you were acting like my mother instead of hers, you would understand what I'm going through." Instead, I opted for the easy way out.

"I'm tired," I told her. "I've been up since seven, and I scouted the entire area. I think bluebirds are a figment of Miss Fletcher's imagination."

I deliberately left out the meeting with Andy. Mom wouldn't like hearing I'd been running around the woods with a boy, and Amy would laugh at some imagined new development between the two of us. Sometimes there really was no point in telling things the way they truly were.

"I saw a bluebird," Amy said after a short silence, stressing the "I." Mom had turned onto Highway 5 and passed the gas station where Matt sometimes worked. I craned my neck for a look, pretending not to hear Amy's remark and its implication.

"I said, '*I* saw a bluebird,'" Amy repeated too loudly for me to ignore.

"Where, sweetheart?" Mom asked. "Erika said she had trouble finding one."

"Just because Erika has trouble doesn't mean everybody does." Amy sniffed. She'd seen me looking for Matt, and I understood the double importance of her remark. Oh, what had happened to my sweet, amiable cousin? I disliked her now more than anybody else in the whole world!

"Did your bird have a blue crest on his head?" I asked, challenging her. "Was he robin sized, with a loud, shrill call?"

"Yep!" Amy stated triumphantly.

"Well, dummy, that was a blue jay!" I told her. I could taste my victory, it was so glorious. "Bluebirds are much smaller. If you ever bothered looking in a bird book, you'd know. You might even have found your own robin instead of needing me to point it out for you."

Mom looked at me in the rearview mirror and gave me one of those pained looks that said, "Really, must you?" My victory dissolved in the realization that she believed I had intentionally started an argument again. Hadn't I promised her I'd be easier on Amy? I looked at her sheepishly. A silence descended on the three of us as we all retreated into our separate thoughts. Luckily we'd reached the mall, and we'd be out of the car soon. Maybe when we started shopping, we could find a new, happier topic of conversation, and the old one could be left behind for good.

Wyckoff Mall was good for that sort of thing. Every time I drove up to that mass of anonymous-looking buildings with their service entrances and truck depots, I got sick at the thought that people could really take a woods or a field and turn it into something as ugly as this. But beyond the first set of double doors was a maze of boutiques, walkways, department stores, restaurants, and indoor fountains. The artificial dazzle and promise of store after store of new spring fashions made me forget all about the out-of-doors.

As soon as we stepped into the first department store and saw those soft pastel clothes on display in the junior department, Amy and I abandoned our fight and pored through the racks.

Amy ran over to the section where denim jeans hung in spring colors of pink, lavender, powder blue, cream, and khaki. Other racks offered jackets and vests, blouses and sweaters, skirts and dresses. A rainbow of sweat shirts and polos filled the shelves. I fingered the materials lovingly, though I knew there was no chance of a new wardrobe this year. Dad's new car had taken up all of our luxury budget, and Mom had given me a choice: either two new outfits or one prom dress. I opted for the dress, and I assumed Amy planned to do the same. So I had to suppress a gasp when Amy held up a pink cotton jacket in front of her.

"Oh, Aunt Mary!" my cousin practically screamed. "Wouldn't this look fabulous on me?"

Mom smiled in agreement. It was true that Amy looked great in pink. But Mom wasn't going to let her buy it, was she? The clothes formed a kaleidoscope in front of my eyes, and I felt myself getting dizzy.

"So can I get these three pieces?" Amy wanted to know. She held a sweat shirt and a pair of jeans up with the jacket.

"Well, let me see." Mom put a finger on her chin. "The jacket is thirty-five dollars, the pants are thirty, and the sweat shirt is how much?"

"Fifteen!" I said with such conviction that both Mom and Amy turned to stare at me.

"In case you're wondering," Amy said, turning her nose up at me, "my dad sent me the money. So don't start getting upset."

"I don't care!" I lied. But of course I did. Once again, Amy was getting something I couldn't have. For a brief, guilty moment, I almost wished my parents were divorced, too, so I could receive checks in the mail from my dad.

"Well, sweetheart"—Mom looked at Amy—

"you're still going to have to choose. Your dad sent only sixty dollars."

"Aww," Amy wailed, sounding a lot like she had ten years earlier at the toy store. "What if I buy a less expensive prom dress? *Please*, Aunt Mary! It's not an outfit without all three pieces."

"Well—" Mom said, thinking it over. "OK, then."

"Great!" Amy flashed her dimples at Mom appreciatively. She probably hadn't given any thought to the prospect of a less expensive prom dress. I knew Mom would forward the extra money from her own paycheck.

Mom must have remembered me at last. She turned and asked, "Would you like something, dear?"

"No, that's OK," I mumbled. We both knew it was what I was expected to say.

After Mom paid for the clothes, we left the department store and headed for France's Formals, Amy clutching the shopping bag tightly to her side. I wondered how she would feel about my borrowing her new things, the way she always did mine. Then I felt bad again for thinking such spiteful thoughts about my very own cousin, even though I found it diffi-cult at times to believe she was my cousin. Between feelings of guilt, envy, and discom-fort about my physical appearance, I was a real mess by the time Mom picked out a pretty lavender dress and held it out in front of me.

"Wouldn't this look great on you!" she said, beaming. I knew she was trying hard, and I didn't want to hurt her. Yet I also knew she must have been thinking about the incident that had just passed.

"I guess," I muttered uncertainly. The dress had an expanse of material that a tall girl like me could carry off. But I felt the low back and V-neck front were better for someone with more of a figure, like Amy.

"Try it!" Mom urged. I agreed reluctantly, more to please her than for any other reason.

It wasn't until I had reached the privacy of the dressing room that I could finger the soft, silky material with real appreciation. After I put the dress on, I examined myself closely. With my pale, unmade-up face and windblown hair, I looked terrible, but I could see that with the right makeup and a fabulous haircut, I could look almost pretty. The idea excited me until I remembered the true facts. Sure, I'd get to go to the prom. If I didn't have a date, Mom and Dad would arrange to have one of their friends' sons take me. But everyone was sure to know he was just an escort, not a real date. A real date could only be a boy I had chosen myself, a boy I really liked. A boy like Matt, the only boy I could even imagine holding me in his arms as we danced across the floor. . . .

I heard voices outside and figured Amy must have run into some of her friends. "Are you dressed?" Mom called to me. "Come out and show us, honey. Some friends of yours are out here."

"I'm coming," I answered her, hoping she was wrong and the voices belonged to strangers.

No such luck. Stepping out into the full light of the store, I saw Jennifer and Matt! It was too late to jump back into the safety of the dressing room. I stood there, humiliated. There was the boy I silently loved, whose embrace I had just imagined, the boy I least wanted to see me like this. I tried to tell myself that it didn't matter, that it was time for me to face facts. It was Jennifer he had embraced the night before, and perhaps Jennifer he would dance with at the prom. Yet, it mattered so much that waves of misery swept over me.

"It looks wonderful, Erika!" Mom exclaimed enthusiastically.

"Yeah, you look nice, Erika," Jennifer agreed politely as she scrutinized my dishevelment.

"You look just like Cinderella." Matt grinned impishly at me.

I knew he meant it as a compliment, but I

didn't miss the double meaning. Wasn't Cinderella the one who picked the peas out of the ashes? Self-consciously, I blinked my burning eyes. In a way Matt was right. I could be Cinderella—but only if he were my prince. No one else thought it was possible, but I knew he'd settle down with one girl, if only I could get his attention. But not looking like this!

A well-groomed woman with neatly coiffed gray hair stepped from behind the counter and walked toward me. "If you like, I'll be happy to take a fitting on the length," she said. "That way, it'll be ready before the general prom rush."

Before I could tell her "No, thank you, I haven't made up my mind," she turned to Matt. "And is this the lucky young man?"

That did it. I couldn't take any more embarrassment. Turning abruptly, I jumped back into the dressing room, my ears echoing from Amy's and Jennifer's giggles and the saleslady's profuse apologies. I took the dress off just in time to hear Matt ask, "Well, there's no law against taking two girls, is there?"

"You'd like that, wouldn't you!" Jennifer said.

By the time I dressed, Jennifer and Matt had gone. The rest of the shopping trip continued dismally. Amy tried on several dresses and looked radiant in all of them. Mom insisted on buying me a cardigan in the same pretty lilac shade as the dress I had tried on.

When I tried to refuse it, Amy said earnestly for Mom to hear, "It's a lot more practical for you than a prom dress." But when my mother walked toward the cash register, Amy grinned wickedly at me.

We drove home through the late-Saturday shopping traffic in silence, nobody saying much of anything. When we got back, I sat on the porch until it was time to help Mom with dinner. After supper Jason came by to pick Amy up for their date, and Mom and Dad went out to a movie. Then I had the whole house to myself. My schoolbooks lay in front of me all evening, but I didn't look at them. Instead, I thought of the shopping trip, the hike with Andy at Otter Pond, and the dress I had tried on for the prom I'd probably go to with a date drafted by my parents. Then I dreamed about Matt and what it would be like to kiss him good night after the prom. And with that, I fell asleep.

Chapter Six

When Monday morning arrived, I dreaded returning to biology. I still hadn't seen my bluebird, and until I did, my project would be incomplete. I knew Miss Fletcher had assigned only common New Jersey birds. She would never believe that I had tried and failed to find one. Andy Chevalier could have told her that I was out Saturday morning looking, but he'd probably also remember that I'd said I had already spotted my bird. I wasn't sure why I had told him that, and I'd feel even worse if I were caught in a lie. In the old days I could have counted on Amy to vouch for me, but at this point she would have told Miss Fletcher I spent the whole weekend in bed, just to spite me.

I didn't think I could feel worse, but when I walked into class and saw all the completed reports around me, I felt like turning around and hiding in my locker. Amy got lucky with that robin outside our window, but what about the others? How could they all be so much luckier at bird-watching than I? I'd seen enough robins, starlings, sparrows, and finches to start a wholesale bird report company. Everything, it seemed, but a bluebird. It just wasn't fair.

I got a break when Miss Fletcher decided to hear the reports in alphabetical order. Bob Adams led with a thoroughly boring and all too long report on the cardinal. Judging by the fidgeting and note passing around me, my classmates seemed to agree.

But our teacher hung on to every word. "How fascinating," Miss Fletcher said when he finished. She looked down her list. "Let's see—Amy Brooks, you're next." She smiled pleasantly at my cousin.

Amy strutted to the front of the room, showing off the outfit she'd bought on Saturday. Then she cleared her throat. "Robin," she announced.

Miss Fletcher beamed expectantly. I wondered if she thought Amy was about to reveal some new, never-known discoveries about one

64

of America's most common backyard birds. If so, she would be disappointed.

"The North American robin is slate blue with a red-orange breast," my cousin began. "It lays three to four pale blue eggs—"

"Did you manage to locate the nest?" Miss Fletcher interrupted enthusiastically.

"Oh, sure!" Amy said, turning to her. "I made it a point to watch them build it. They even used a few strands of my hair." The extra bit of drama made a real impression on my teacher.

"That's marvelous!" Miss Fletcher praised as she scribbled in her grade book.

Amy finished her report and sat down.

Andy's was the only name in the class that started with C. When he got up and announced his bird, a chorus of soft groans arose. Andy spent ten minutes giving a very long list of the measurements and habitats of the house sparrow, a bird even more common than the robin. I stifled a yawn and reflected that Andy had reverted to the same old, boring brain he always was. If I'd thought he was any different at Otter Pond on Saturday, it was a serious mistake. Andy went on with his dull report, while people shifted impatiently in their seats.

"In recent years the house sparrow, which is not native to this country, has crowded out other species—the eastern bluebird for example—"

My ears perked up when I heard "bluebird." What was it Andy had said? My eyes looked up and met his. He was looking straight at me! I quickly averted my gaze. The incident on Saturday was just a chance meeting on a homework assignment, but once again I felt a blush creeping up my neck and face. I was sure every eye in the room was on me. But when I sneaked a glance around, everyone else was fidgeting restlessly or gazing out the windows.

Matt Duncan's name came up next. "Coming, Fletch," he called out, sliding out of his desk in one neat movement. Matt was one of those boys who couldn't really stand still. Every muscle in his well-formed body seemed to ripple and be ready to go. Shifting his weight back and forth on his feet, he began, his wavy blond hair falling forward over his forehead.

"Crows," he started. "Black feathers; principal food—popcorn; wingspan—"

"Wait a minute," Miss Fletcher interrupted. "What did you say was its primary food?"

"Popcorn," said Matt. A short silence was followed by dispersed giggling. Andy Chevalier would have gotten sniggers, but Matt got giggles.

"Can you substantiate your claim, Matt?" Miss Fletcher asked, challenging him.

"Sure," he said. "It just so happened that a couple of crows joined us at baseball practice on Saturday morning."

When Miss Fletcher didn't look convinced, he went on.

"For a while it looked like they were going to help out in left field. But, Miss Fletch, we discovered the crow doesn't catch balls very well."

"Matt!" our biology teacher admonished. "This is not a creative-writing class. If you would get on with the crow's particulars, I would appreciate it. So, I suspect, would the rest of the class."

I couldn't speak for everyone else, but I was enjoying Matt's speech. He was so entertaining—and so handsome to look at there at the head of the class. His blue eyes smiled mischievously at his own little jokes, and his skin glowed from a fresh new tan, the first of the season. I shot a glance at Jennifer. From the look on her face, I could tell she was in love, too.

"As the crow flies," Matt agreed. It made no sense, but the class burst out laughing. Even Miss Fletcher smiled.

"Now, what about that popcorn?" she asked.

"After baseball practice, I discovered the crows had broken open my bag of popcorn and eaten it all." Matt looked at Miss Fletcher as clear-eyed as a little boy. "If that isn't proof they eat popcorn, then I don't know what is."

"What about before there were humans to pop it for them?" someone called out.

"The cavemen had fires, didn't they?" Jason spoke up.

"They hang out on my uncle's farm eating the grain," Bob put in. Then things got out of hand.

"Class. Quiet, please!" Miss Fletcher held out a hand. "What does this tell us about crows? Amy Brooks? Do you know?"

"That they're big eaters?" Amy offered.

"I'm looking for a particular word." The teacher pointed at Andy.

"Opportunistic," Andy said neatly. As usual he'd known all along.

"That's right. The crow is opportunistic," Miss Fletcher agreed. "It's a scavenger, meaning it eats whatever is available, even if it means stealing other birds' food."

"I'll kill the dirty thieves!" Matt said, joking. "That was good popcorn."

"Thank you." Miss Fletcher dismissed him. "That's enough. Next? Susan Eckhorn."

And so it went. My turn would be coming up after Wendy Houseman. The clock said 11:02, and that meant there were only thirteen minutes to go. I hoped Wendy's report would last until the end of class. I was doing everything I could in my mind to buy some time. But no such luck. Wendy's house finch report was over at 11:10. There was no avoiding it now. My turn was up.

Miss Fletcher looked at me expectantly. "Well, Erika? Let's hear about your bluebird."

"Ehh—" I pretended to go through my papers. "I—uh—"

"Did you do your homework this weekend, Erika?" Miss Fletcher questioned me sternly.

I felt my face go red. Of course I'd done my homework. At least I'd tried to! If only I hadn't been such a wise guy and told Andy I'd seen my bird. He would have been the perfect person to help me if my pride hadn't gotten in the way. Now I was stuck. "Sure!" I made a last attempt to buy some time. "It's just that, uh—since the bluebird is such a special bird, I'd like to take a little more time with my report." I looked at the clock. It was 11:12. "I mean, I don't think there's really enough time left to do it right, do you?"

Out of the corner of my eye, I thought I saw Andy look at me. Amy knew what my problem was and suppressed a snicker. Matt gave me a sly wink as if he were privy to some kind of secret. His glance added to the warmth that was already creeping up over my face right to my scalp.

But my last-ditch effort for extra time worked. The bell rang. Instantly, books and kids flew to the door. "All right, Erika." My teacher smiled. "You win. We're having a special film on reptiles tomorrow, and there's an assembly on Wednesday. But you'd better be ready to give your report on Thursday."

I got the message. Miss Fletcher would be accepting no more excuses. Grateful for the reprieve, I glided out of the room.

Chapter Seven

After school I stopped by Joe's Franks, hoping to see Matt. I knew it was nearly hopeless, but I couldn't break the habit. It even looked as if he and Jennifer really might be serious about each other—at least he didn't seem interested in any other girls.

Matt did arrive—dragged through the door by Jennifer. I wondered if she had let go of his hand all day long. My pulse quickened as Matt caught my eye and winked, then pulled away from Jennifer to walk toward my stool.

"Great job in class, kiddo," he said, clasping my shoulder. "You know, you just may have more spunk than I ever gave you credit for."

"Gee, thanks," I answered stupidly as he walked back toward the booth Jennifer had saved for them. My shoulder burned under the imprint his warm hand had left behind.

I drifted back to reality and glanced around Joe's. Amy and Jason sat snuggled together in the seat opposite Matt and Jennifer. All the other booths were filled with twosomes caught in the rush of spring fever. The couples who were squeezed out of the booths huddled close to one another at the counter.

Feeling out of place, I left the diner, making my way down the hill on Main Street. Maybe I'd try looking for that bluebird again. But if I hadn't succeeded all Saturday and Sunday, how did I expect to do any better in a couple of hours after school?

"Hello, Bluebird!" A familiar male voice caused me to whirl around in surprise. It was Andy, running breathlessly to catch up with me. He was wearing a yellow cotton sweater that I hadn't noticed in class. It made his dark eyes and hair stand out. I thought he looked taller than before, too, but that couldn't be possible. People didn't grow taller over the weekend. I felt suddenly frightened just like on Saturday. "Why are you calling me bluebird?" I snapped.

Andy's enthusiastic smile faded. "I'm

sorry," he mumbled, his confidence faltering. "It's just that, well, sometimes your eyes are kind of blue. And since that's the bird you're working on, I—"

I felt myself warming toward Andy, but at the same time I was trying to fight that feeling. What would Matt and Jennifer and Jason and Amy think if they saw me talking to him? They thought he was a joke. But they were still at Joe's and wouldn't see us. And there was no law that said I couldn't be polite.

"I see," I said evenly. "I guess I don't really mind if you call me that. But you can call me Erika, too, you know."

"Erika," Andy repeated, saying my name as if it were some kind of precious metal. He smiled. "OK, Erika it is."

I smiled back. Jennifer's words of a couple of weeks before came flying back just then: "I think he likes you." At the time I'd shrugged the remark off, assuming she was trying to tease me. Now I wondered if she was right. But could I ever make myself like him? Could I ever fall for a guy who used only big words and always walked around with his head in a book?

"Erika," Andy said once again as if testing the sound of my name, "how is your ornithology report coming along? Because if you still need help—"

Now Andy sounded just like his stuffy old self again, asking questions about school, trying to be superior. Part of me really did want to ask for his help, but another part of me wanted to prove I could do it by myself.

"It's just fine," I lied. "It's just that there's too much going on at home for me to be able to do much in the way of homework."

It wasn't the truth, not totally. But to my surprise, he said, "I figured something was wrong." He said it with such real concern that I could only stare at him for a moment.

"You did?" I finally returned.

"Sure," he said. "It's not hard to figure out what happened in biology class. You were practically Miss Fletcher's favorite student until Amy asked to be her helper."

I laughed. "I don't care about that," I told Andy. "If Miss Fletcher wants to give Amy that old shoe box to pass around, it's all the same to me."

Andy grinned back at me. "That isn't the greatest privilege I can think of. But I think there's more to the story."

I didn't answer. Discussing Miss Fletcher was one thing, but my private life was quite another. It didn't seem right. Yet in a way I was eager to tell Andy what was really going on. I needed to talk to the kind of person who would never repeat what I told him, no matter what kind of outrageous things I said. Andy wouldn't even have the chance. But then would he really understand a problem that wasn't intellectual? I didn't know.

We had wandered into Patterson Square, a small park named after one of the original Swedish settlers who had founded Jefferson Township. Andy pointed to a bird that had landed on the ground in front of us. He held a finger to his lips to warn me to be as quiet as possible. At first I hoped it might be a bluebird, but as we crept closer, I saw dowdy brown feathers.

"A cowbird!" Andy said excitedly.

So what? I thought, disappointed.

But Andy went on. "There's a fascinating story about that bird," he said, smiling knowingly at me.

"What?" I pretended to be interested.

"Well," he began, "the cowbird lays eggs, but she doesn't bother building a nest. She doesn't even hang around to feed her babies or see how they're doing. She lays her eggs in another bird's nest. Usually she picks a bird that has smaller babies than she does. That way, when her babies hatch, they throw the others out of the nest and hog the foster mother all to themselves."

"But doesn't the other bird know they're not her babies?"

75

"Why should she?" Andy pointed out. "They're in her nest, aren't they? Often, too, the baby cowbirds are so big, it's all the foster parents can do to get enough food to meet their demands."

"Oh, that nasty bird!" I said indignantly. "It's just not fair."

Andy laughed. "That's one thing you have to learn, Erika. Life isn't fair. It's nature, that's all."

I glanced over at Andy curiously. Was he trying to tell me something, or was this just another bird story? I let it pass for the time being. We had come to an old, abandoned mill that stood at the edge of a small falls. The pounding water sent a fine spray back to us and wet our hair. The sensation of the soft mist on my face felt good, and I began to smile.

Andy looked at me and smiled, too. In that moment the tension between us melted away, and I no longer felt the need to look away from his searching gaze.

Andy spoke first. "I'm not really experienced in this field, Erika," he said, even more intense than usual. "But you're different from the other girls in school."

"You're different, too," I added hastily, then immediately regretted my response as I recalled how often he had been taunted for his difference.

If he noticed my awkwardness, he ignored it as he went on. "I mean, I can't imagine talking to another girl like this, or even walking in this park with her. Do you understand?"

I nodded. But Andy hadn't finished yet. "In fact, I was wondering if you'd like to get some ice cream with me tonight. My dad said I could borrow the car."

Andy was asking me for a date! I hesitated, wanting impulsively to say yes. Then the anxious feeling returned, and I said quickly instead, "Oh, that would be nice, Andy, but Mom wants me home tonight." I glanced at my watch. "I really should get going now, in fact."

But I was sure Andy hadn't missed how I'd brushed him off. He smiled shyly as he turned from the falls. "Come on," he said. "I'll walk you part of the way."

Suddenly I didn't want to go home. I wanted to stay with Andy. But it was too late to change my mind.

He took my hand and led me away from the park. We walked silently for a few blocks, just as we had in the woods two days before. Now I was the one who wanted to say something, and I just couldn't. Conflicting feelings choked my voice. I did want to be with Andy. In the brief time we had spent together, I felt more calm and secure than I had since all the trouble at home had begun. But it was too late to change my mind about the evening.

As we approached the intersection of Maple and Franklin streets, so did the bus that would take Andy home. He gently touched my arm and whispered, "Goodbye," then ran swiftly away. I began to think about Andy. How little I knew about him. What were his mother and father like? Did he have brothers and sisters? And what about the farm where he lived? For I remembered he did live on a farm. Did it have cows and horses, apple trees and cornfields?

For years we had shared classes, and I had never thought about the most basic details of his life. Now I wanted to know all about him. My curiosity startled me.

Andy jumped on the first step of the bus, then turned to wave. "You should come to my house sometime," he shouted. He didn't say when. I just nodded as the doors closed behind him.

Chapter Eight

On the way home I stopped at the Greenway Supermarket to pick up a carton of orange juice. As I was walking out, a jumble of notes tacked on the bulletin board inside the entrance caught my attention. Some of the messages asked for furniture, cars, or appliances to buy. Others wanted to sell. A yellow tabby cat had been found on Harrison Lane. Someone was offering a reward for a green and blue parrot lost near Hicks Street. A parrot. Instantly my brain started working. These messages were read by lots of people in Jefferson Township who shopped here. Maybe even bird-watchers. Ripping a scrap of paper from my notebook, I wrote this message:

"Wanted: whereabouts of eastern bluebird. Please call 352-7068."

When I got home, the house was in an uproar. Dad had come home early and was now paging nervously through the newspaper. Mom was sitting on the living room sofa drinking coffee and looking nervous as well.

And to my surprise I saw Uncle Bob, Amy's dad, pacing the room like a caged tiger. He hadn't been in our house more than two or three times since he and Aunt Carol had been divorced years ago. What could he want now? I said hello, and they all jumped up instantly, then sat down just as fast when they saw me.

"Amy's usually home by now," Mom said to no one in particular. "Oh, Erika, do you have any idea where she might be?"

"Sure," I said. "She's probably still with Jason at Joe's. I left there not too long ago." I didn't mention a thing about where I'd been in the meantime, but no one asked, either.

"We have to keep an eye on her and those boys," Uncle Bob growled. "That girl is getting too wild."

To my surprise I jumped to Amy's defense. "Amy's not wild! She's having some Cokes and hanging out with friends. Anyway, Jason's a good guy. You don't have to worry, Uncle Bob."

Mom threw me a grateful glance. I wondered at myself. Was that really me defending Amy?

"I'm going to go get her right now," Dad announced. Immediately he left the house. We all listened in silence as he started the car in the garage and quickly pulled out of the driveway.

Uncle Bob turned to me with a grin that looked slightly forced. "So, how are you, sweetheart?" He patted my shoulder. "My, haven't you gotten tall! You take after your dad, don't you?"

"I guess so," I answered uncertainly. It felt kind of strange, talking to him about family resemblances when so much time had passed since I considered him part of the family.

"You know why I'm here, don't you?" Uncle Bob asked, squeezing my shoulder. I squirmed to get away but couldn't.

"Uh—no," I said, struggling for an excuse to leave the room. "If you don't mind, I have to get my—"

He ignored my attempts at freedom. "I'll bet quarters have been a little cramped around here lately. But after today, you'll have your own room once again. Amy's coming home with me."

Now the conversation had gotten interesting. I was no longer in such a hurry.

"But I thought it was all set that she would live with Aunt Carol!" I protested.

Mom threw a warning glance in my direction. Uncle Bob's arm tensed on my shoulder, and his face hardened.

"Nonsense!" he growled. "Has that girl ever had a chance to make a decision for herself?"

Mom said nothing, and I freed myself from my uncle's embrace.

I didn't like his rough tone. From the way Mom fidgeted with her wedding ring, something she did whenever she got really nervous, I had the feeling it wasn't the first time he'd yelled that afternoon.

Mom turned to me in a distracted way. "How was school, honey?"

"Fine," I answered. I knew she was simply changing the subject. If I had told her how school really was, she wouldn't have heard it in the state she was in. For once, I didn't mind too much.

We sat in dead silence until the car returned a few minutes later. Through the window I could see Dad and Amy in the front, both staring grimly ahead. Another vehicle followed them into the driveway—Matt's red pickup! Matt and Jason hopped out quickly. Jennifer wasn't with them.

The door opened, and Dad and Amy

entered through the hall. Uncle Bob ran forward and gave her a bear hug. "Hi, sweetheart!" he said. "Haven't you gotten tall!"

His words were practically the same ones he'd said to me. Perhaps he'd only been practicing for the real thing. But my cousin's reaction to her father was certainly different from mine. She seemed to hang on his every word.

"Really, Dad?" She beamed under her father's attention. "I'm only five-three. Erika's the tall one." She smiled in my direction almost wistfully. Did Amy actually envy me for being tall?

Over her shoulder I noticed Matt and Jason standing in the hall, waiting uncertainly for the right time to come in. It was the first time I'd ever seen Matt look unsure of himself. The situation was awkward, and I was surprised Amy had invited them to come along. I guess she might have wanted Jason's support in case the visit with her father went badly. But I had no idea why Matt had come. *Where was Jennifer?*

Finally Mom spotted them. "Why don't you boys hang up your coats and come in?" she told them. Then, turning to Uncle Bob and Amy, she said, "You two should go and talk in the den. I'll make some more coffee. Erika, why don't you come with me and get some Cokes for the boys?"

Jason and Matt came in, and Dad immediately engaged them in a conversation about sports.

In the kitchen I got the drinks in silence, while Mom brewed another pot of coffee. It was all too much for me—Amy's dad, then Matt, sitting right here in my own house. But I knew that this time it was equally difficult for Amy.

Mom broke the silence. "You know why he's here, don't you?" For a funny moment I thought she meant Matt, and my face flushed. But of course she meant Uncle Bob. I looked at her. "He came to get Amy, right?"

"Yes," Mom agreed. "He wants to convince her to go and live with him instead of Aunt Carol."

"Can he do that?" I got some ice out of the freezer. "Do you think she will? She's complained for years that he never really pays any attention to her. Except for checks, that is."

Mom made a face. "If she does, it'll break your aunt's heart. Amy's her only child, and I'm the only one she'll even trust that girl with. But Amy's growing up, Erika, and she's the one who'll have to make the decision."

"I'm glad I'll never have to make a choice like that," I told my mother. "You and Dad will always be together."

Mom smiled and patted my cheek the way she had when I was a little girl. "Yes, we will. But you'll have your own decisions to make, too," she told me. "It's part of growing up. I'm sure you'll be ready when the time comes."

My cheek felt warm where she had touched me. I felt as close to her as ever in that moment. It gave me a boost of confidence. And I sure needed that to face the boys.

Fortunately the conversation was still sports when I returned to the living room, and it was easy to listen to Matt relate the adventures of Jefferson High's practice on a muddy baseball field. After about ten minutes Uncle Bob and Amy opened the door to Dad's study and came out. Everyone looked at them curiously.

"Will you stay for dinner?" Dad asked Uncle Bob.

Uncle Bob shook his head impatiently. "I've got some business to get back to." After a hasty goodbye, he was gone. He never even allowed Amy to introduce Jason and Matt. But I suppose that was too much to expect.

Amy looked like she might cry. Mom put an arm around her and squeezed her gently. "Go sit down, honey. I'll start the supper," she said, retreating to the kitchen.

"Would you boys like to stay for dinner?" Dad asked.

They accepted. After both boys called home, Jason and Amy settled down to watch TV, her soft blond hair falling on his shoulder as he cradled her in his arm. I wondered if Jason would have any influence on Amy's decision to live with her mom or her dad. Uncle Bob lived about twenty-five miles away, out of the Jefferson High school district but close enough for Amy to see Jason on weekends. But if Uncle Bob really thought Amy was getting too wild with boys, he might restrict her dating, maybe forbid her to see Jason altogether. Aunt Carol trusted Amy a lot more than Uncle Bob did, but in California there would be no chance for her to see Jason at all.

I watched my cousin and her boyfriend as they snuggled together on the couch. Jason had lasted longer than Amy's other flings, and she really did seem to care for him. Perhaps she really was in love this time. But now circumstances threatened to separate them forever. I felt a sudden burst of pity for Amy. I never had Matt, and the pain of not ever having him was bad enough. I could only imagine what it must feel like to lose someone you really loved.

As dinner progressed, Amy and Jason became more engrossed in each other, whispering things that no one else at the table could hear. Mom didn't usually let even Amy get away with that, but this evening Mom was so involved in conversation with Dad that she didn't notice at all.

I sat silently across the table from Matt. How many times I'd dreamed of this very moment. Now that it was here, I was lost. Where was Jennifer? Why had Matt decided to stay for dinner? Could I hope he had stayed because he finally had noticed me? But it didn't seem appropriate to ask about Jennifer, so I pretended to be absorbed in my meal. I cut each piece of meat slowly and carefully, not daring to lift my head and meet Matt's glance. The longer I gazed at my plate, the more self-conscious I became.

Eventually I'd consumed all the meat I had, and all the new potatoes, and all the carrots and green beans. When I could avoid it no longer, I looked up. Matt was staring at me. A hot flush coursed up my neck and rose right to my scalp.

"Are you a baseball fan?" he asked, his eyes bearing down on me.

I looked down at my plate again, feeling shy and miserable. "I have been since I was a kid," I told him.

"Hey, I'd like to see you at some of the Jefferson games," he said.

You would? I thought, wanting to scream

the words. Aloud, I said, "I think the team's good this year."

"We're going to go all the way—that is, win the championship," he said boastfully. "But only if our fans cheer us on."

We were talking so easily now. Months of waiting and hoping finally meant something. Matt talked and listened eagerly, as if this conversation were the most important thing in the world to him. All my prayers had been answered. Matt finally cared. Or did he? Jennifer's face kept popping into my mind as we talked, spoiling everything. How would she feel if she knew he was here?

He stopped talking just long enough to serve himself more potatoes. When he turned back to me, he grinned broadly. "You know, Erika, I really like the way your hair looks."

I raised my hand to my head to smooth down what up to that moment had been my uneven haircut. At the same time I realized Mom and Dad had overheard his remark. They both looked up and threw us amused glances.

As Mom began to clear the table and Dad brought in dessert, Matt whispered to me, "I was really impressed with the way you handled yourself in Fletch's class today. You fooled her like an expert. I didn't know you had it in you."

"I wasn't trying to deceive her," I explained, feeling a bit defensive. "But I'm glad I've got a few extra days. I looked all over for my bird, but I couldn't find it."

"You mean you actually went looking for it?" Matt's face registered incredulity. I felt as if I'd just been handed the bozo-of-the-year award. "Why don't you just fake it and save yourself lots of time and trouble?"

"I can't do that," I said.

"Why not? I did," he said, smiling. "You think I really give two cents about crows? I'd just as soon leave all that bird nonsense to cuckoos like Andy Chevalier."

"Andy's not a cuckoo!" I burst out. "You don't really know him." Again I surprised myself. First I had defended Amy, now Andy. I wouldn't have guessed I could do either a week earlier.

Matt didn't seem to want to pursue the thought. "Suit yourself." He shrugged. For the first time all evening, Amy and Jason seemed to notice our presence. I wanted to snatch back my words and begin again. My big chance had arrived, and I was about to blow it by defending Andy Chevalier!

The spell had been broken. Matt jumped up to help Mom clear off the table. She smiled at him, impressed by his good manners. Suddenly I thought about Andy and the enthusiasm he had for learning and discovery. Even though I hadn't found my bluebird, I'd learned a lot in my search. It wasn't a waste of time. Andy's attitude made a lot more sense to me than Matt's.

Matt's remark bothered me. It was the first chink in the perfect suit of armor I'd put him in. I couldn't help but wonder if there were any more.

"Why don't you kids go out for a while?" Mom suggested after we'd finished cleaning up.

"I'm game," Matt said, looking directly at me. "What do you say, Erika?"

He was asking me to go with him! I looked down at my clothes: a plain pair of navy cords, boots, a long white and blue sweater. Nothing special, certainly not the clothes I would have planned to wear for our first date. But Jason and Amy were already walking toward the door. There was no time to change, no time to put on makeup, no time to do anything but say "Sure."

"Drive safely, Matt," Dad said as we headed toward Matt's truck. "You're carrying some precious cargo there."

"I'll say!" Matt agreed enthusiastically, giving me a wink.

Amy and Jason exchanged knowing glances. *How many times have they heard Matt say the same kind of thing?* The thought spun through my head as we walked toward Matt's truck.

Chapter Nine

We all squeezed into the cab of the pickup truck, with me pressed close to Matt. His arm felt strong and warm through his flannel shirt, and he smelled of spicy after-shave. This was what I'd imagined all year, but it didn't feel the way I'd dreamed it. My mind flashed on the image of Matt and Jennifer in Joe's booth. Had that been only that afternoon, just a few hours earlier? I had no idea what had happened between them, and I wasn't sure I wanted a boy who could float so effortlessly from one girl to the next.

I tried to push such thoughts out of my mind as we pulled into the parking lot of Peggy's Frozen Delights. We were hardly an item yet, after all. Matt had simply asked me out;

my parents had even suggested it. But Matt did jump at the chance; he must have wanted to be with me, whatever the reason. Worrying would only spoil this opportunity.

So I laughed along with the others as we entered the ice-cream parlor. Amy seemed to have forgotten her dad's visit entirely as she and Jason slid into a booth and put their arms around each other. I got into the other side with Matt. To my surprise he took my hand and held it tightly.

"Amy is lucky to have a cousin like you." He smiled broadly.

I never expected to hear a friend of Amy's praise me. "Huh?" was the only response I could manage.

"Sure," Matt assured me, his cheeks dimpling as he grinned. "She tells Jason and me all the time. She wouldn't know what to do without you. She's crazy about you."

Amy couldn't get by without me? It was so unlike anything Amy would say, I had to wonder if Matt was telling me the truth. Another dark thought entered my mind. He might want to lie to me, to flatter me, to make a big impression, if he'd brought me along for ulterior motives.

Before I lost my nerve, I had to ask, "Where's Jennifer? She's not sick or anything, is she?"

A cloud passed briefly over Matt's face, then he snickered. "A guy's got to get out on his own sometimes, doesn't he?"

I glanced at Amy. She read my look and announced a sudden need to go to the bathroom. Of course I said I'd go with her. Matt and Jason thought nothing of our departure and went on scanning the ice-cream menu.

"What's with Matt?" I asked Amy once we were safely behind closed doors. "Where's Jennifer? How come he's paying all this attention to me all of a sudden?"

Amy didn't come back with one of her usual flip answers. She bit her lip nervously, as if she might be hiding something, then busied herself with her lipstick, pretending not to be able to talk.

"Tell me the truth," I demanded. "When I saw Matt with Jennifer this afternoon, he didn't look like a guy who'd be interested in another girl. What's going on?"

Amy looked at me sheepishly. "You're not going to like it."

"What I don't like is being left in the dark."

Amy leaned against one of the sinks. "I should have said something earlier, I guess, and not have gotten your hopes up." She looked down at the floor. "He and Jennifer had a fight."

"Did they break up?" My curiosity was aroused.

"Not exactly," Amy said. Slowly she raised her eyes and looked me in the face. "It was more like a lovers' quarrel. Jennifer really wanted his class ring, and I think he might be getting nervous about it. But she's probably sitting home by the phone right now, waiting for his call."

Meanwhile, my heart was pounding, and I was breaking out in a cold sweat. My worst suspicion was true. "So he's using me to test his feelings for Jennifer. He doesn't really like me, does he?"

Amy frowned. "Matt can sometimes be a jerk when it comes to other people's feelings, Erika. Awhile back I told him you liked him. I'm sorry. And you're pretty and bright, just the kind of girl he loves to be seen with. And he *has* been asking about you lately."

I looked at Amy. She had abandoned her act entirely. Could her father's visit have affected her?

"Don't worry," I said. "It's all right. It's not your fault he's the way he is. Anyway, I'm sure he could've seen I liked him himself. I was pretty obvious."

It was a funny thing for me to say, considering I'd just seen my dreams of Matt crumble away like a sand castle. But Matt didn't seem quite as important as this flicker of humanity I'd witnessed from my cousin. Maybe we could be good friends once again.

I forced a smile. "What do you say we get back out there? I feel a hot fudge sundae coming on."

She smiled back. "Sounds great."

When we returned to the booth, there was a banana split waiting for me. "I thought you might like it, so I went ahead and ordered one," Matt said. I noticed he had one, too.

"Thanks." I tried to smile. I hated bananas. Of course Matt didn't know that, but then he hardly knew me at all. I realized I hardly knew him, either.

Matt was too busy trying to butter me up to notice that I only picked at the dish. "You look great," he said, a few moments later. "Did anyone ever tell you what neat-looking eyes you have?"

"Not really," I answered. Amy caught my eye then and smiled wryly. But I didn't need to be reminded not to fall for Matt's flattery.

"Have you ever worn that sweater before? It looks great on you," he went on. I'd worn it a million times, but of course Matt wouldn't have noticed that. I suppressed a giggle.

A few weeks earlier I would have been overwhelmed by the situation, memorizing Matt's every word, pouring layers of meaning on every glance he gave me, every time his hand brushed mine. Now I only wanted to survive the evening and get safely home.

But Matt was clearly in a boisterous, rowdy mood and continued to talk. If he noticed that Amy was unusually silent, or that I was definitely not fascinated by him, he never let on.

"Say, isn't that Megan Griggs in that booth with Steve Petrie?" he asked loudly at the end of a dissertation on the importance of second-base strategy in baseball. "Boy, she's looking good these days," he added in a voice Megan and Steve could certainly hear. "Of course, we've got the two most beautiful ladies in the place right here in this booth." He winked at Jason and grabbed me around the shoulder. I could only smile weakly.

I never could have had a comfortable relationship with Matt, knowing I'd always have to keep one eye open for the inevitable next girl. Matt just wasn't interested in any commitments—not even to Cinderella. I wished I'd realized this months ago. As it was, I felt sorry for Jennifer. She certainly had her hands full.

As we were getting ready to leave, Matt pointed to the door. "Hey, look, Erika, there's your friend the cuckoo bird."

I turned around in the booth. Andy was standing at the front counter!

I slumped down in the booth. I couldn't let him see me. He'd know I'd lied to him. I couldn't imagine spending an entire evening with him, but I didn't want to hurt him. He was a genuinely nice person. After the way things had gone that evening, I almost wished I'd accepted his date in the first place. His sweet dullness couldn't have been worse than Matt's egotistical conversation.

"Come on, Erika," Matt said. He grabbed my hand and yanked me off the bench. There was nothing I could do now. Maybe, though, I could slink by Andy without his noticing.

I kept a step or two behind Matt, using him as sort of a protective shield. My ploy might have worked—if Matt hadn't gone and opened his big mouth.

"Hey, Andy!" Matt grinned. "I didn't know bookworms liked ice cream."

Andy stared at Matt, clearly at a loss for words. But I could tell he was angry. I couldn't believe Matt's insensitivity.

Then it happened. Andy saw me. The expression on his face changed. He frowned, and I could see his chin quiver slightly.

I tried to make the best of it. "Hi, Andy," I said, smiling.

He gave no indication of seeing the affection I was trying to convey. He still looked hurt.

I realized I was trembling as we walked out to the parking lot.

Chapter Ten

When we got back to the house, Amy and Jason got out of the car and walked over to the porch steps, where they continued the hugging and kissing they had started in the car. I didn't want to step over them to get into the house and put Mom and Dad on the alert, so I waited in the truck with Matt, feeling awkward and confused. Matt leaned over and grinned at me.

"How about a friendly little good-night kiss?"

I looked at his face and froze. The streetlight was shining right into his eyes, giving him a funny expression I'd never noticed before. I almost wanted to laugh, thinking of how horrified he'd be if I told him I'd never been kissed by a boy before. But I felt tense and unhappy. I'd dreamed of Matt's kiss for months, and now that I could make it happen, I wasn't so sure I even wanted it.

"Come on, Erika. You know you've been thinking about this moment."

"I—I don't know—" I began to say. I had been thinking about this for longer than Matt could guess, and suddenly all these doubts were creeping into my mind. First, an image of Jennifer came into view, sitting forlorn and dejected by the telephone. Then another face replaced hers—Andy's. I couldn't forget how hurt he had looked seeing me at Peggy's Delights with Matt after I'd turned him down.

I reached for the handle of the car door. If Matt's kisses were meant for me, they'd come again.

But I moved too late—I felt Matt's warm breath against my neck. Then he was kissing me! I was trapped in the moment I'd always dreamed of. But the tingles I still half hoped for didn't happen. I struggled to get away.

"Hey—what's your hurry?" Matt asked as I jumped out of the truck. Dad must have heard something because the porch lights flicked on, and Jason and Amy jumped, too.

Inside, as I took my coat off, I heard Matt's truck drive off, the roar fading gradually to a hum. I thought of the kiss Jason and Amy had exchanged. It had looked so good.

Amy was already in our room by the time I got upstairs. She was sitting on her bed, staring forlornly out the dark window. She turned around when she heard me enter the room. "Hi," she said and grinned at me as if it hadn't been less than five minutes since I'd seen her.

"Hi." I smiled back at her.

"I'm sorry about tonight," she stated flatly.

"You already told me," I said. "Really, Amy, there's nothing to apologize for. In fact, I'm glad tonight happened. Maybe I'll finally get Matt out of my system."

But Amy was only half listening. "I've been doing a lot of thinking," she announced.

"Yeah, you didn't look like you were always with us at the ice-cream parlor. Do you want to talk about it?" When she didn't answer right away, I added, "Remember when we were kids and you used to run up here and cry on my bed whenever you had a problem?"

"We're not little anymore," she said sadly. "And the problems aren't so simple. Sometimes, Erika, you don't realize how lucky you are."

"Me?" I plopped down on my bed.

"Don't act so surprised. Sure, you're

lucky. You've got a mom and dad who love you—"

"Hey, don't pull that 'poor Amy' stuff on me. Your parents love you, and you know it."

"Do I?" She was starting to cry.

"Of course you do. Look, Amy, I know the divorce has been really tough on you, and maybe it is easier for me having both my parents in the same house. But your dad wouldn't have come tonight if he didn't care about you. And I've never seen a better mom than Aunt Carol."

"Then why did she go and marry someone on the other side of the world and change my entire life without even talking to me?"

In that moment I became aware of the hurt and pain Amy had been experiencing. I *had* been lucky. Caught up in my boy craziness, I had never noticed that Amy had to cope with a far more serious situation—probably since long before her mother's remarriage.

I didn't know what to say, but I felt I had to do something, so I walked over to Amy's bed and hugged her. To my surprise she grasped me fiercely and held on as she let months of suppressed tears flow freely.

We stayed like that for several minutes. Then, her tears exhausted, Amy fell back against her pillows. "I thought everything was settled, but now I don't know." She threw up her hands in despair. "Dad wants me to live with him."

"I know," I said.

"But Mom's expecting me as soon as final exams are over."

"And now you don't know who you want to stay with," I finished for her.

She nodded. "I don't know if I really want to live with Dad, but I'd be closer to Jason."

"How much does he mean to you?" I meant Uncle Bob, but Amy didn't take it that way.

Her cheeks glistening with tears, she sighed deeply. "I like him better than any other boy I've ever gone out with. I don't want to lose him, Erika. But I really miss Mom, too, and I want to be with her wherever she is. But if I move away, I'll never see Jason again!"

I put my arm around Amy again. "Don't worry," I said. "I know it will work out for you." As confused as I was myself, it was the only thing I could think of saying. I held my cousin until she fell asleep, then I crept softly back to my own bed.

Chapter Eleven

That night I had the strangest dream. I was in school—in biology—when Miss Fletcher turned into a crow. Standing at the head of the class, she scolded, "EriCAW, EriCAW! Where is the report on your bluebird, EriCAW!"

The other kids in the room had turned into birds, too. They started fluttering around and taunting me, repeating over and over, "Your bluebird. Where is your bluebird, EriCAW?" Matt was a blue jay, but he tried to confuse me by changing into a bluebird and then back into a blue jay again.

The taunts of the class finally drove me outside to Otter Pond Park. There I struggled up the hill and through the undergrowth, hunting for something. I stopped when I came to the eagle's nest. The mean-looking bird looked as if it were going to swoop down on me. The huge wings spanned seven feet above my head. I screamed and ran away, crashing through the undergrowth.

Then I looked up and no longer saw the enormous bird above me. I saw instead a tiny bird with a red breast and a blue back—a bluebird. My fear turned to happiness as I kept telling it, "I've been looking for you, I've been looking for you." The bluebird then changed into Andy, but I wasn't surprised. He fell to the earth and put his arms around me, and I just kept on telling him, "I've been looking for you for such a long time."

When I woke up, it was still pitch black outside, and I lay there in the darkness, thinking. I was surprised and a little embarrassed by the dream. I remembered the times over the past months when I had made fun of Andy or laughed with the rest of the class over some remark he had made. And when he had called me "Bluebird," what a face I'd made! Would he ever forget that? Or the time at Joe's when I dashed out without an explanation—and also left him with the check! Or that time at Otter Pond Park, when he'd shown me the eagle. I blushed, remembering how Andy's arm around me had caused such mixed feelings in me that I'd pulled away from him. Now I understood those feelings very well. I'd begun to like Andy even then, without realizing it! A new thought filled me with fear. Did Andy still like me or had the incident at Peggy's made him give up on me? Maybe I'd been blind for too long. He had probably decided that I *was* just like the others. Maybe he'd fall for someone else soon—somebody nice and pretty and smart, who'd appreciate the real Andy.

I slid back beneath the warm covers. The dream had long faded, and I lay there, trying to recapture the wonderful sensation of the eagle changing into a bluebird and the bluebird changing into Andy. The darkness outside became steadily lighter, and the first bird of the morning began to sing. I wondered if it could be my robin, the one I had saved from near death outside my window. I thought of Andy again. He was tall and thin, and yet so strong, so balanced. I thought of his excitement when he showed me the eagle. I remembered his shy, friendly smile when he told me the bluebird stood for hope, love, and happiness.

Hope! The word shouted out at me. If Andy once liked me, then maybe he would again. I would be nicer to him in school. I'd go out of my way to talk to him. I'd admit I never did find that bluebird, and never could without his help. I'd—I'd even tell him how much I liked him.

With that I drifted back to sleep.

When I awoke again, the sun was streaming into the room, lighting up the white muslin curtains like Chinese lanterns. It shone on Amy's makeup mirror and sent a shaft of light up to the ceiling of the room. Particles of fluff from the red mohair sweater I'd lent Amy caught the breeze and drifted across the rays of light. Everything possessed an unreal quality.

As the details of my dream flooded back to me, the mess in the room didn't bother me one bit. It looked like the aftermath of a happy party.

Throwing aside the covers, I sat up in bed and stretched my arms up to the ceiling as far as they would go. "It's good to be alive!" I sang out loud. "It's a beautiful day!"

Amy opened up one sleepy eye and looked at me questioningly. "What's with you?" she grumbled.

"Get up!" I instructed her. "The day's too gorgeous to sleep away. You'll be late for school."

"Is this the same Erika Johnson I used to know?" Amy questioned me suspiciously. "The grump?"

"Look who's talking," I accused her. At the same time I felt a little ashamed. Maybe I, too, had been difficult to live with, childishly obsessed about neatness and chronically depressed about Matt.

"Erika," Amy insisted, "you haven't exactly been the most happy-go-lucky person I've ever known, you know." She could still read my mind, after all that had come between us.

"Maybe you're right," I admitted. "But today is going to be different. Ever since last night, I've had a hunch—"

"Uh-oh." Amy untwisted herself from her covers and walked to her bureau. "I was afraid this was going to happen."

It was my turn to be puzzled. "Huh?" My cousin reached for a bathrobe. "You know what I'm talking about," she admonished me. "Or rather, who."

Had I been talking in my sleep? "What do you mean?" I wasn't ready to talk to anyone about Andy yet. Not until I talked to him myself.

"Matt!" Amy stared at me knowingly. "I knew you'd end up falling for him. Please, Erika. Believe me for once. He's just too immature to be good for any girl."

It took a minute for her words to sink in.

111

"*Matt?* Really, Amy. Is that why you think I'm in such a good mood?"

If Amy thought I'd been out of character before, now she must have thought I was just plain weird. But she didn't seem to mind. "Sure, sure" was all she said before heading for the bathroom.

That's when I remembered I wanted to wash my hair to look nice for Andy. I dashed out into the hall ahead of her, and we were in a mad race for the bathroom.

"Whoa, there!" said Mom, whom we almost knocked over on the way. But she heard us laughing, so she didn't bother to stop us. When we got to the shower, I jumped in first, but Amy got to the faucets, turning them on full force. My pajamas were soaked.

"They were ready for the laundry anyway!" I gasped, nearly drowning upright in the stream of water.

"The joke's on you!" Amy yelled back, still laughing. "I wasn't going to take a shower anyway. I took one last night. I just wanted to cool you off about Matt."

"You are one big rat!" I accused her. "I told you I don't care about him anymore!"

Mom chose this moment to stick her head in the door. "I'm glad to see you girls are finally getting along!" she said. We all laughed, and I sprayed Amy with a shake of my wet head, getting her a little damp, too.

After we got to school, Amy headed for the cafeteria to look for Jason, while I started toward the stairs to the basement locker room. I usually saw Andy walk by during the morning, but this day he was nowhere in sight. It was funny how things like that happened. When I didn't need him, he always seemed to be underfoot. But now when I wanted him, he was nowhere to be found. I badly needed to explain what I'd discovered and to find out if he really cared for me the way I thought he did.

My dream had lifted my spirits, and something inside me hinted that it wasn't too late—not yet, anyway. But where was Andy? If he didn't show up before the homeroom bell, I'd have to wait until biology. Then I might become too unnerved to talk to him at all. I grinned to myself. I had found my bluebird. But what would Miss Fletcher say if I told her where?

Two boys from the baseball team, Bob Carter and Ted Wilson, passed me in the hall on the way to the senior lockers, which were the only ones situated on the first floor. They glanced at me briefly, Bobby sending me a quick wink. Next to Matt Duncan, they were two of the cutest boys in school. Any other day I would have been thrilled with Bobby's attention; but that day I just responded with a simple smile, as if the wink were the most natural thing in the world. Even Ted and Bobby didn't seem so terribly special anymore.

I went down the stairs to the basement locker room, still hoping at every turn to see the familiar dark eyes, the tall, slim figure. As I remembered how he had held me at the park, little shivers of excitement ran up my spine. *Be patient*, I told myself. *Don't spoil things with a second boy. Move carefully.* If kids laughed, let them. I no longer cared that Andy wasn't one of Jefferson High's stars. He was special enough for me.

A hand intercepted me at the bottom of the stairs. I felt a shock go through me—could it be him? Then I saw the broad, grinning face, the wavy blond hair. It was Matt!

"Hi, beautiful!" He smiled at me.

"Hi," I answered. *This is crazy*, I said to myself, amazed at the difference a day made. *Matt's stopped to talk to me, and all I can think about is getting away.*

"What's the matter?" he asked, pouting. "Aren't you happy to see me?"

"Oh, sure," I lied. "But I haven't even been to my locker yet. There're a few things I've got to get."

"Hold on!" Matt drew me out of the crowd of kids pushing us from all sides and safely leaned me against the wall. "The first bell hasn't even rung yet."

"Oh, hasn't it?" Jill Lobel passed us and threw me a funny look. Did she think I was trying to steal Jennifer's boyfriend? As if I wanted to!

"Hey." Matt lifted my chin with his finger. He might as well have been any other boy in school. I didn't feel any of the tingles I used to feel when I was around him. *Why didn't you do this earlier, while I was still in love with you?* I accused him silently.

"That was great ice cream last night, wasn't it?" Matt said.

"Not bad," I answered politely. He had never noticed how little I had eaten.

"Well, I can top that." Matt grinned. "What do you say we join Amy and Jason on Friday for a real dinner? We'll go someplace romantic like the Town and Country. The food's not bad there. It's time we retired Joe's to the freshmen."

Obviously, he'd been to the Town and Country before. But I couldn't believe he'd actually asked me out. He was talking about a real date, not a casual get-together as the night before had been. I had to hand it to him—he was persistent. No wonder he always got what he wanted.

More kids noticed us. Jessica Cole and Debby Watson gave us a look that said clearly, "Oh, brother, he's at it again." Some sophomore girls looked envious. A few of Matt's friends passed and grinned. Everyone was curious to see who Matt Duncan was working on next. This time the lucky girl would be me—if I wanted it.

I, meanwhile, was looking everywhere but at Matt. I still felt a little vulnerable around him. I must have stared at the crowd for about a minute without answering. Matt was growing impatient. "Well," he said, "what about dinner? When should I pick you up?"

"Matt," I said, "I really do appreciate the invitation. It's just that I already have plans. I hope you understand." The words sounded to me as if they had come from someone else, but I felt relieved.

Matt stared at me in surprise. I wondered if any girl had ever turned him down before. He'd have a stroke when he found out I had picked Andy over him.

"Suit yourself," he grumbled. He looked a little awkward, as though he didn't know how to behave after being rejected.

"Listen," I said impulsively, "I don't know

116

what happened to Jennifer. But I heard she misses you."

"Sure," he mumbled, though he seemed to relax a bit. "Well, how are you going to spend Friday night? Hunting for your bluebird?"

I looked Matt straight in the face. He wasn't a bad sort of boy, but he definitely was not my type. "No," I said, smiling. "Friday will be too late. But I hope to find him soon." Then we were off to our separate lockers before the first warning bell sounded.

Chapter Twelve

Before biology I had gone back to my locker, so almost everyone had arrived at class by the time I did. I shot a glance at Andy just as he was sliding into his front-row seat. He caught my gaze, but instead of holding it, he diverted his eyes to something outside. Was he just contemplating a homework assignment, or was he hurt about the night before? I couldn't be sure.

Matt let out a whistle as I walked by, and I smiled back at him out of habit.

Jennifer Kelly looked at me as I walked into class, and I wondered how much she knew. I felt a little sorry for her. She was so pretty, much more so than I. But seeing the insecurity in her big blue eyes as she looked up at me told me a different story. Loving the most popular boy in the junior class carried its own set of worries.

I could put her at ease immediately about me, though. Matt was quickly joining the ranks of ex-crushes stored in the back of my mind. Seeing him and Andy together in the same room confirmed that. A lot of my desperation for Matt had been tangled in the general web of confusion I'd felt about myself all year, about my popularity with boys, my doubts about my attraction for boys, my jealousy for Amy. But Andy was different; just contemplating his sensitivity, his intelligence, his warmth settled so many of my inner conflicts. If only I just had an opportunity to tell him so!

The final bell rang, and I slid quickly into my seat. Miss Fletcher walked in and, out of breath as usual, hastily scribbled "reptiles" on the blackboard with one hand while she pulled off her sweater with the other.

"I'm afraid, class, that the wrong film arrived," she began. "So we're just going to discuss reptiles in class today without a film. We will, however, continue with our reports on Thursday as I said yesterday." Miss Fletcher threw a meaningful glance my way, and Matt winked at me once again. I hoped Andy hadn't seen.

"Which group is more closely related to

the dinosaurs?" Miss Fletcher asked. "Reptiles or birds?"

It was typical of her to start off with a weird question like that. A murmur went up from the class. Matt spoke up first. "Reptiles used to be dinosaurs," he said. "That's why cavemen were always hiding out in caves and building huge fires. Nowadays they blow up shots of reptiles to make them look like dinosaurs in movies."

It sounded plausible enough—until I realized cavemen lived long after the dinosaur era. But Matt still had that talent for convincing people. Only a few people raised their hands to contradict him.

I looked over at Andy. He sat with that patient look of his. But he didn't bother to correct people the way he usually did. He didn't seem to care at all whether birds or reptiles were related to dinosaurs.

"Erika," Miss Fletcher called. "Are reptiles cold-blooded or warm-blooded?"

"Cold-blooded?" I guessed. I hadn't thought much about that sort of thing.

"Amy," our teacher addressed my cousin. "Are birds cold- or warm-blooded?"

"Warm-blooded," she guessed correctly.

"Jason," Miss Fletcher asked my cousin's boyfriend, "are dinosaurs cold- or warm-blooded?"

"Cold-blooded," he answered. A murmur of protest went up from the class.

"Didn't they discover dinosaurs to be warm-blooded?" Jill asked.

"That's right." Miss Fletcher beamed at her. "So which group is related to them? The warm-blooded birds or the cold-blooded reptiles?"

"Couldn't evolution have turned the reptiles' blood cold?" Matt wanted to know. "You're not going to convince me that birds are related to dinosaurs just because they both have warm blood. What about me? Isn't my blood warm?"

"Boiling!" Jason called out. "Especially when you're with a certain species."

Everybody laughed. I looked over at Andy and noticed a wry grin on his face. Certainly he knew the real answer very well. Why didn't he say anything?

When the laughing died down, Miss Fletcher raised an eyebrow and looked in his direction. Yet Andy remained uncharacteristically silent. Not once did he glance at me. The happiness and anticipation I'd felt all morning gradually faded away, replaced by anger at myself and a lump that knotted my throat. Andy did not look or act like a boy who was in love—especially with me! My earlier eagerness seemed foolish. Of course Andy wanted nothing to do with me. I had learned the truth too late. And I had lied to him as well as to myself.

"OK, OK, that's enough!" Miss Fletcher waved her hands at the class. "Will you please put on your thinking caps for once?"

When no one had a reply, she pointed in Andy's direction. He had been gazing out the window, and his reply sounded mechanical and uninterested. "Birds are believed to have descended from dinosaurs. Feathers have been found to have evolved from scales," he said. "Some primitive birds have feathers that still closely resemble scales. The cormorant still lacks oil in its feathers and must dry its wings after diving."

For a minute the class remained silent at this piece of information.

Then Matt broke the peace. "Holy flying reptile! Those feathered friends sure tricked me!" Instantly the class shrieked at Matt's remark. It became Matt, not Andy, who finally established that birds were related to dinosaurs. But Andy didn't seem to care. In fact, he seemed to have tired completely of the whole game.

When the bell finally rang, I gathered up my books in anticipation. We'd have time to talk now. But Andy headed for the door without once looking in my direction. I bolted after him, nearly pinning Matt against the bulletin board in my haste. "Whoa!" he said. Jennifer immediately jumped to his side, casting a suspicious glance in my direction. Andy was already way ahead in the hall, but I managed to catch up.

"Hi!" I mustered up all the cheerfulness I could.

Andy turned around. His eyes were dull and held no sign of the spark I had seen the day before. He looked like someone who's stayed up all night studying.

"Hi," he returned listlessly. The old despair that I'd felt so often with Matt flowed through me now.

"How's that eagle?" I asked hesitantly. "Been back there yet?"

"No," he replied flatly.

"W-well—" I stammered. "I thought maybe we could sit together at lunch. I'd like to talk to you about bluebirds and things. And, uh, I owe you a root beer."

He looked at me curiously. A tentative glimmer lit his eyes but died quickly.

"I've got to write up a report in the library" was all he said.

I tried to stop him before he continued down the hall.

"Andy!" I pleaded. "Can't we talk for a few minutes?"

Andy looked at me with his most blank expression. Then I saw what looked like anger light up his eyes.

"About what?" he asked.

"I want to explain! Last night wasn't what you thought."

"It doesn't really concern me," he retorted. "Meanwhile, this bookworm has a lot of work to do."

I stared as he disappeared down the hall. What was I doing, almost pleading with Andy to love me? Wasn't he still Andy, the class bookworm?

In my desperation to have a boyfriend, could I have fabricated an Andy who didn't exist, an Andy based on a silly dream?

Despondent, I made my way to the cafeteria. A snapshot of Andy in the Otter Park Reserve flashed into my mind. No, I had seen the real Andy, I was sure of that. Perhaps he was still there but hidden from me. I had to find a way to lure him out once again, to show him that the real Erika had been in hiding, too—but was here to stay now.

Chapter Thirteen

When I got home that afternoon, the house was in an uproar. Suitcases that had been brought out of the closet lay open on the living room couch and coffee table. Piles of Amy's clothes stood stacked next to them waiting to be packed. The washer and dryer were both running at full speed. It was then that I remembered that Amy had been absent from eighth-period English. At the time I'd been too full of thoughts about Andy to be concerned.

I walked toward the laundry room, calling, "Anybody home?"

Mom peeked out from behind a pile of ironing. "Oh, honey, it's you." She smiled, dabbing at her forehead with her sleeve. It was hot in there.

"What's going on?" I demanded. "Why aren't you at work? What are those suitcases doing all over the place?"

"Erika!" My mother beamed. "You'll never guess the good news!" She went on before I even had a chance to guess. "Aunt Carol called today. She's settled in Santa Monica and wants Amy to join her immediately. We're putting her on a flight tonight."

"But what about school?" I asked. "And Jason? She's finally found someone she really likes."

"Oh, honey." Mom gave me a look. "The school says they've dealt with this type of situation before. She can actually finish everything but a couple of exams through the mail, so we'll see her in a few weeks. And I don't think there was much of a choice between Jason and her mother. Of course, I told her she was welcome here anytime."

Mom went back to ironing one of Amy's cotton blouses and spoke without bothering to look up. "Life is strange sometimes," she said mysteriously. "Things don't always turn out as you might expect. But the important thing is that Amy will be back with her mother. Amy has missed her terribly."

"I know," I agreed. Her words stuck in my

mind: Life *was* strange sometimes. Now I wasn't sure I even wanted Amy to go. I could use her help with Andy.

"What are you thinking about?" Mom asked.

"Nothing." I wasn't ready to tell my mother, not just yet. But I went on. "I'm happy for Amy. But you know something funny?" This time I didn't give my mother a chance to guess. "I'm going to miss her. That love seat's going to look weird all made up."

Mom laughed, then bent down to fold the blouse. "Go see if Amy needs any help packing," she instructed.

I found Amy in our bedroom, leaning over the love seat to get a better view through the opened window.

"What are you looking at?" I asked.

She whirled around when she heard me. Her pale face and red, smudged eyes were telltale signs she'd been crying. But she smiled now. "She won't leave the eggs," Amy whispered.

I leaned over her shoulder and looked out at the branch of the oak tree where the robins had their nest. Sure enough, the robin I had rescued days before was sitting in the nest, patiently warming and guarding the eggs she had laid in her new nest.

"Parenthood is some job," Amy commented. "They'll be at it all day, and after they're born, those selfish kids will never be satisfied."

I made a face. "Would you be if all you got were worms? Ecch!" But when Amy turned to face me, tears rolled freely down her pink cheeks.

"Mom cut short her honeymoon to send for me." She reached for a tissue. "She said she couldn't stand to be without me anymore. I was afraid she'd be thrilled to have me stay here with Dad."

Impulsively I turned and hugged her. My gesture brought even more tears. But through them, Amy gave me the biggest smile I'd seen from her in years.

"I sure hope you find your bluebird, Erika," she said. "Watching those robins really meant a lot to me. You know what I mean?"

"I know," I said. And I did. I was only sorry it had taken such pain for us to understand each other again.

"Erika," she continued, "I know I haven't been the best cousin to you lately—coming in here and taking over your room, putting you down in front of the other girls. I just want to let you know I'm sorry. You deserve better." This time she hugged me.

I didn't know how to reply. "What if I send

you pictures of the babies?" I asked through my own sobs, then we both laughed at how silly we looked.

An hour later Amy was packed and ready. Dad came home early from work to bring Amy to the airport, which was a good hour away. Mom and I were helping load her luggage into the car when the phone rang.

Amy ran for it. I wondered if word had spread that she was leaving. She had only had time to tell Jason.

"It's for you!" Amy called out to me. "Did you put an ad on the supermarket bulletin board?"

I nodded to her as I reached for the phone. "Hello," I answered shakily. It was silly that I should tremble when I picked up the phone. But in the back of my mind I was praying that it might be Andy.

I was soon disappointed. An older man was on the line. "Are you the young lady looking for a bluebird?" he asked.

"Yes, I am," I replied.

"I happen to have a nesting pair on my property. You're welcome to stop by anytime to have a look."

"Oh, thank you," I told him. I couldn't suppress a sigh of relief. "You see, it's for a report in school, and so far I haven't been able to locate any in Jefferson Township."

I heard a chuckle at the other end of the line.

"Young lady," the man said, "there is only one pair of bluebirds in all of Jefferson Township, and they are right here in my orchard."

"Are you sure?" I asked. Miss Fletcher said she had assigned only common backyard birds.

"Why don't you stop over tomorrow morning early, before school?" the man suggested. "Then you'll be sure to catch me at home and the birds will be active. You can catch the school bus later." He proceeded to give me directions to his farm.

"Who is Mr. Chevalier, anyway?" Amy asked after I'd hung up. "He had a nice accent. Is he Andy's father?"

"Mr. Chevalier?" I felt my face go pale. That had to have been Andy's father! "Is that who it was?"

"Erika, really!" my cousin chided me. "You act like you saw a ghost. Andy isn't that bad. So what did Mr. Chevalier want?"

I grabbed another suitcase and headed out to the car. "Looks like I've found my bluebird" was all I answered before I gave Amy one last, fierce bear hug as she stood next to the waiting car.

Chapter Fourteen

"Isn't that pretty," Mom said as she took the Route 1 exit off Highway 32. We were driving to the Chevalier farm. Flowering trees had burst into bloom everywhere, and although it was only six in the morning, no one could doubt any longer that spring had really come.

"What, Mom?" I asked absentmindedly.

"The dogwoods. I'd almost forgotten how beautiful it gets around this time of year."

"Oh. Yeah," I answered. But my thoughts had turned back to Andy. In a few minutes I'd be seeing him. It was certainly his dad who'd called the night before. Amy said he'd asked for me by name, and Andy's father was an ornithologist. Probably the only person in Jefferson Township besides me—and Andy—

who knew about bluebirds and knew that they practically no longer existed.

"Mom," I said. "You know how we take certain things for granted?"

"Mmmm," she answered. We were driving along Route 1 now, and the scenery was breathtaking. Dandelions and buttercups added a burst of yellow to spring fields, and wild flowers of every color lined the roadside. Birds sang from the telephone wires above our heads, and a fresh scent of spring wafted in through the window.

"Well," I continued, "some things just seem to be there all the time, and you don't even think about them until they're gone. Then you have to go hunting for them. And when you find them—if you do—they feel more precious than before."

"My!" Mom looked over at me with a smile. "That's quite a mouthful for so early in the morning. Is there something that led up to this?"

It was my turn to smile, but I couldn't really be sure of anything—not quite yet.

"I'm not sure, Mom. If you don't mind, I'm not quite ready to explain it yet. It has to do with the bluebird, you might say."

"Well, I'll be waiting!" Mom exclaimed. Then in a more serious tone, she added, "Listen, honey, there's something I've been meaning to say."

"What, Mom?" I asked, but I sensed what she was going to say.

My mother sighed heavily before she went on. By this time we had made the left turn onto Lucas Road. "I guess I haven't been much of a mother lately," she said.

"Oh, no, Mom!" I protested, but she cut me off.

"Oh, yes," she corrected me. "This whole thing with Amy just got out of hand, and at your expense, too. I think I should have realized that I was sacrificing my own daughter to try to help my sister's."

"Mom, really!" I protested. "You make it sound so terrible. I was the rotten one."

"I wouldn't say I was terrible, but certainly unfair." Mom smiled faintly. "I've never told you this, but when Aunt Carol and I were growing up, I was the favored child. Since then, I've felt terribly guilty about it."

"But it wasn't your fault," I pointed out.

"I know," Mom agreed. "But I felt obligated to let Amy stay with us. I know it was a big inconvenience to you."

"Forget it, Mom," I said. "We still have a couple of good years together. You can make it up to me."

When she started to laugh, I added, "You

know, it's going to be very different without old Amy to share a room with. Do you think Aunt Carol will let her come back this summer?"

"I never thought I'd hear you say that!" Mom cried.

She'd pulled up in front of a white Victorian farmhouse. The building must have been a hundred years old, but it was well maintained. A field of young alfalfa behind the house swayed gently in the early-morning breeze.

A man got up from the porch and waved at us. He was tall and thin like Andy. His head was covered with thick, white hair.

"Good morning!" he called out, walking toward the car. I noticed a faint French accent again.

"Didn't you say a classmate of yours lived here, Erika?" Mom asked.

I nodded silently. Andy was nowhere in sight. Well, at least I would get my report done.

We got out of the car, and Mr. Chevalier came up to us, extending his hand. "So you are Erika! André has told me about you. You want to see some bluebirds?"

André? I thought to myself. He was so much more interesting than I'd ever suspected—and so modest about it. *And he told you about me?*

Mom chatted with Mr. Chevalier, then left to drive back home to get ready for work, and Andy's dad took me out back to a small apple orchard. "André's been out there since dawn setting up," he explained.

Sure enough, Andy was crouched down low in the grassy orchard, putting some last-minute adjustments on the binoculars, the same ones he had used to show me the eagle's nest. I was actually excited about the prospect of finally seeing the bluebirds.

Andy smiled uncertainly as I approached. "Hi," he said softly.

"Hi," I answered. All the speeches I had rehearsed since the night before fled my mind.

Andy's father cleared his throat. "You two go ahead with your observations," he said. "I've got a couple of reports to catch up on. Why don't you come up to the house in a few minutes for some breakfast?"

"Great," both Andy and I agreed in unison, and then we both laughed out loud.

"À bientôt!" Andy's dad told us. Then he was gone, his long strides taking him back to the house until he disappeared from view altogether.

"Is he French?" I asked.

"French Canadian," Andy said. "So am I, as a matter of fact. I was born in Quebec. We moved here when my mom died."

Your mom died? My mind reeled with questions. *How come you never told anyone about your background? Can you forgive me for being so foolish? Can you tell that I like you? Do you like me, too?* But it seemed so much easier to stick to impersonal questions for the time being.

"So you knew all along I hadn't found a bluebird." I looked up into his face. He smiled gently in response and nodded his head.

"Poor old Miss Fletcher has been spending too much time in school to realize that some birds just aren't as common as they used to be," he said. "I think she'll be upset to learn that only one nesting pair remains in all of Jefferson Township. There wouldn't be any if my dad hadn't put up this special birdhouse to attract them."

The long awaited bluebird fluttered to its nest as we were talking. A large green grasshopper dangled from its mouth. Four hungry mouths instantly popped into view. Through the binoculars I could see the pink of their large beaks.

We watched them for several minutes, while Andy pointed out facts that I jotted down in my notebook. But one question still plagued me. If this beautiful little creature was indeed a harbinger of spring, a symbol of hope and happiness, why wasn't it common anymore? Why had the bluebird left Jefferson Township? Andy seemed to sense exactly what I was thinking. He took my hand and led me to a telescope he had focused on the hills beyond. "Look!" he commanded.

Through the viewfinder I saw what he was pointing at. The megalopolis was rapidly descending on Jefferson Township, New Jersey. Land that had once been extensive woods and farms was now only shopping malls and developments. Ugly, gray concrete patches encroached even on Otter Pond Park in the distance, the home of so many wild creatures, including one bald eagle.

When I pulled back from the telescope, Andy's eyes looked sensitive and troubled as they gazed questioningly into mine. A breeze picked a lock of dark hair off his forehead.

"Erika," he began, "do you ever get the feeling, as you get older, that there is less and less beauty in this world to love and enjoy?"

I'd never heard Andy—or any boy, for that matter—say anything like that. Yet, when he said it, I recognized my thoughts of the last couple of days—Andy and I had a lot more in common than I had ever let myself suspect.

"Yes," I agreed. I hesitated, then plunged in again. "But at the same time, other equally wonderful things are making themselves known to me. Don't you have that feeling, too?"

The troubled look left Andy's eyes as he stared at me with an intensity no boy had shown me before. "Yes," he answered simply.

Then, before I had time to think, he took me into his arms and pressed his lips softly against my hair. And then against my lips. This was the kiss I'd dreamed of for so long! The kiss was so spontaneous that it left us both breathless and shy, gazing at each other with the wonder of new discovery. But Andy still appeared to be wrestling with conflicting feelings that weren't yet fully resolved for him.

"Erika, tell me you're not playing games with me," he begged, holding my hands and looking intently at me as he spoke. The early-morning sun shone directly into his face, and I saw that Andy was a boy who needed to be cared for as much as any Matt Duncan.

"I didn't always realize I liked you," I told him honestly. "And I'm so sorry I treated you badly. But you're the only boy I can think about now."

He smiled and kissed me tenderly on the lips before we walked hand in hand to the house to have some breakfast.

Chapter Fifteen

On Thursday, the day after I saw the blue-birds, biology class was in an uproar again. Miss Fletcher announced our homework—the chapter in our books on worms. "This will give you some background for Friday, when we'll be dissecting them."

"Gee, I never heard of cleaning the bait instead of the fish," Matt called out.

The class laughed, but as usual our teacher was not amused. "That will be enough, Matt," Miss Fletcher said sternly. "Do you realize we're two days behind the rest of the biology classes? I suspect that may be partly attributed to you. How many times have I had to call the class to order after one of your outbursts?"

141

Matt grinned sheepishly. Jennifer shook her head at him, her dark ponytail gleaming. She'd really managed to rewind him around her little finger, I observed. No other girl had been able to do that with Matt before. I suspected she owed me some thanks.

"Now let's continue our class reports on birds," Miss Fletcher said, looking in my direction.

Matt was about to call out something when a warning look from Jennifer shut him up. Andy smiled knowingly. I clutched the report in my hand.

"Well, Erika," said Miss Fletcher, "if you still haven't finished your report, I'm afraid I'm going to have to give you an incomplete."

Everyone froze for a second. Then I announced, "I have it."

The class cheered as I got up. "Way to go, bluebird!" Matt yelled out. Jason let out a whistle.

"That'll be enough, class," Miss Fletcher warned. "Let's hear what Erika has to say."

I walked nervously to the front of the class, clutching my report. Normally I hated to give oral reports. My words often spilled out all over one another as I grew more and more aware of the eyes on me. It was especially bad while I was in love with Matt; I was so afraid he would make fun of me.

Sensing my discomfort, Andy smiled encouragingly to me and gave me a secret thumbs-up sign. I relaxed and began to regain my confidence. This was going to be the best report Miss Fletcher had heard from this class.

I cleared my throat. "The eastern bluebird," I announced. "Until May first, this bird seemed to me to be extinct in Jefferson Township." Miss Fletcher looked surprised, but I continued. "On May second, Wednesday, I discovered one nesting pair on the Chevalier farm off Lucas Road."

A few kids looked over at Andy curiously. He just smiled up at me. Since Amy was gone, nobody in class knew about us yet.

"The eastern bluebird is approximately seven inches long," I continued. "The female is duller than the male. He is bright blue above with a rusty red breast and white belly. The bluebird's main food is insects. It nests in the cavities of trees or fenceposts. . . ."

"Thank you, Erika," Miss Fletcher said proudly when she thought I had finished. "That was well researched and most informative."

"Wait!" I protested. "I'm not done. The best part is yet to come."

"By all means, continue," my biology teacher said. She managed a puzzled smile.

Pushing back a wisp of hair that had escaped from her bun, she leaned back against the blackboard, folding her arms in front of her. Andy grinned broadly as I went on.

"There's a good reason why I couldn't get the report done until now," I ventured boldly. "The nesting pair that I observed on Andy's farm are really the *only* bluebirds left in Jefferson Township!"

Miss Fletcher protested. "Erika, do you know what you're saying? The birds I assigned to this class are common eastern backyard birds. I've used this list every year."

"It's true," Andy called out. "My father's an amateur ornithologist, and he can confirm it." In the past, Andy had often contested other students, but never Miss Fletcher herself.

While our teacher stood speechless, I continued. "The bird Jason did his report on is partly responsible. The starling came from Europe a hundred years ago, and it's driving the bluebird out of its nesting sites."

"Go ahead, blame my best friend," Matt pretended to grumble. Everybody laughed.

"And then, the fields and woods around here are disappearing." I turned to Miss Fletcher. "Did you know that the bluebird is considered to be the symbol of love, hope, and

144

happiness? It would be a shame to lose such a beautiful creature."

"Oh, dear, yes," she said. "Now it's doomed to extinction, too?"

"No!" I protested. "We don't have to let it be. Andy's dad has a great idea for a project, if you'll let me explain it."

"Go on," she said, one eyebrow raised in anticipation.

"Well," I explained, "Mr. Chevalier has the plans for a type of birdhouse that will bring bluebirds back but keep English sparrows and starlings out. I'd like to distribute the plans in class and get people to build them and hang them in their backyards. It might be good for students who need to get some extra credit." Miss Fletcher nodded in Matt's direction. I went on. "We can bring bluebirds back to Jefferson Township; there's still hope."

I didn't mention anything about love and happiness; that was my special secret, mine and Andy's, that is.

Chapter Sixteen

Five weeks later Jefferson High held its junior prom. Andy arrived to pick me up, looking tall and handsome in a black tuxedo. I had picked out a pink carnation for him to wear, and I pinned it proudly on his lapel. Mom and Dad took some snapshots with the new Instamatic, then we were off.

Andy's Dad had lent him the car we had used to deliver bluebird boxes to all the Jefferson Township residents who had responded to a notice we had placed in the Jefferson Township *Bugle*. Already a new nesting pair had been sighted, bringing the total to four adult birds. Professor Chevalier was writing an article about the experiment for the newspaper, and Miss Fletcher had given anybody who helped us build them extra credit. But now the old Ford was washed and polished, ready for a different kind of mission.

The parking lot at Jefferson High was full of cars when we got there. Kids were dressed in their finest. Jennifer and Matt spotted us and came running over.

"Oh, Erika, what a dress!" Jennifer gasped when she saw me. "It's beautiful!"

"It's the dress you saw me try on in the store," I said. "Remember?" *Remember when Matt said there was no law against taking two girls?* I added to myself.

Jennifer didn't say anything, but I could tell she remembered. The look on her face showed me how much I must have changed and grown up in the past few weeks. I didn't look or feel like the same self-conscious girl I was then. Andy had had a lot to do with it. Or, as he would say, he helped me see the good qualities that were lying dormant in me all along.

But if Jennifer was surprised by my appearance, it was nothing compared to the shock she next experienced. "Oh!" she gasped when a familiar-looking blond came into view. "What are you doing here?"

"Going to the prom with Jason. Just like we'd planned. I had to come back to take a couple of exams I couldn't finish by mail."

I had been talking on the phone regularly to Amy about some of the classwork she just couldn't understand through the mail. Finishing the year by mail seemed preferable to spending just a few weeks in a new high school.

During one of our scheduled calls, Amy told me her mom said she could come out a week early to go to the prom with Jason.

She swore Jason and me to secrecy, and we managed to make all the necessary plans for her. I hadn't even told Andy, with whom I now shared almost everything in my life.

Amy looked at Andy approvingly and smiled broadly. Of course, I'd shared with her everything that had happened, a little hesitantly at first. To my surprise she'd been delighted for me.

"He's a good one," she said. "Guys like him can be counted on. They're interested in relationships, not flings. Sometimes it's not easy to tell who's got it."

Now she smiled at him. "You look great," she said.

Andy grinned confidently. "Especially with the right girl," he said, putting his arm around me.

"I'll second that," Jason said, doing the same with Amy.

"Oh, Jason!" Amy turned and kissed her boyfriend on the lips. "You're wonderful!"

"I'll second that," I said, laughing as I stretched up to kiss Andy. Then Jennifer kissed Matt, now her confirmed boyfriend.

Everybody laughed, and then we all went inside.

Andy and I held each other close through the first dance. All I could think was, *What if I'd never seen through to the real him? What if I'd always gone along with the idea that he was just a boring brain?*

Andy seemed to be thinking the same thing. "You know when I first started noticing you?" he whispered in my ear as the music carried us around the room.

"Mmm—when?" I murmured against his neck. It smelled of cologne.

"Last semester when we were studying plant biology."

"Oh, all those wasted months!" I held Andy closer.

"Nothing's wasted now that we're together." Andy stroked the bare skin of my back, where the dress was cut out. "But you want to know something funny?"

"What?" I snuggled closer.

"I always thought you went for those he-man types. I never dreamed I'd have a chance."

"You're silly." I smiled. "Why, all along you were the boy for me. It just took me awhile to see it."

The song was coming to a close. I reached up and met Andy's lips, and we kissed a long time. Andy pulled away just enough to look down at me. Then he held me again and whispered softly, "This world is getting to be one great place, Bluebird."

Caitlin

From Francine Pascal, the creator of the SWEET VALLEY HIGH® books, comes something new and very exciting. It's CAITLIN: A LOVE TRILOGY and you won't want to miss it!

Caitlin — she's gorgeous, charming, rich and a little wild; she's the outrageous, dazzling star of LOVING, LOVE LOST, and TRUE LOVE. You're going to want to read all three —just to see what Caitlin will do next as she reaches out for her heart's desire!

For readers who like lots of excitement with their romance and lots of romance with their excitement — CAITLIN: A LOVE TRILOGY! Get it wherever paperback books are sold!

Bantam Books

SPECIAL MONEY SAVING OFFER

Now you can have an up-to-date listing of Bantam's hundreds of titles plus take advantage of our unique and exciting bonus book offer. A special offer which gives you the opportunity to purchase a Bantam book for only 50¢. Here's how!

By ordering any five books at the regular price per order, you can also choose any other single book listed (up to a $4.95 value) for just 50¢. Some restrictions do apply, but for further details why not send for Bantam's listing of titles today!

Just send us your name and address plus 50¢ to defray the postage and handling costs.

SWEET VALLEY HIGH

☐	25033	DOUBLE LOVE #1	$2.50
☐	25044	SECRETS #2	$2.50
☐	25034	PLAYING WITH FIRE #3	$2.50
☐	25143	POWER PLAY #4	$2.50
☐	25043	ALL NIGHT LONG #5	$2.50
☐	25105	DANGEROUS LOVE #6	$2.50
☐	25106	DEAR SISTER #7	$2.50
☐	25092	HEARTBREAKER #8	$2.50
☐	25026	RACING HEARTS #9	$2.50
☐	25016	WRONG KIND OF GIRL #10	$2.50
☐	25046	TOO GOOD TO BE TRUE #11	$2.50
☐	25035	WHEN LOVE DIES #12	$2.50
☐	24524	KIDNAPPED #13	$2.25
☐	24531	DECEPTIONS #14	$2.50
☐	24582	PROMISES #15	$2.50
☐	24672	RAGS TO RICHES #16	$2.50
☐	24723	LOVE LETTERS #17	$2.50
☐	24825	HEAD OVER HEELS #18	$2.50
☐	24893	SHOWDOWN #19	$2.50
☐	24947	CRASH LANDING! #20	$2.50

Prices and availability subject to change without notice.

Buy them at your local bookstore or use this handy coupon for ordering: